# SHADOW RUNNER

by
## Michael Martins

*Dedicated to Shannon, Ethan,
and Chico Roberto*

# CHAPTER 1

**M**ARCH 18<sup>th</sup>, 8:42pm

Pepito and Marta stood under a tall, ornate lamp in the parkette at the northeast corner of the Plaza de Armas, the main square in the heart of Cusco, Peru. It was Friday night and the usual cluster of tourists had gathered around the benches.

Pepito felt the brisk wind pierce his tattered sweater, it was too small - barely reaching his wrists. Maybe he would get a new one for his birthday. Or maybe he would get the new Peruvian national team soccer jersey. Better not to get his hopes too high, he thought. He flicked his dark bangs from his eyes. He scanned the crowds. He heard Portuguese coming from the group closest to him. "Brazilians," he thought. They are friendly but usually tight with their money. He kept scanning. The next group was a dozen or so Japanese; they too were typically welcoming, but communicating with them was often difficult and awkward.

He kept looking. Over Marta's shoulder he spotted what looked like university students and he could hear English between their bursts of laughter. Pepito turned to Marta, "Let's try them." Marta followed him as the two strolled across the parkette with their wicker boxes in hand.

"English?" Pepito questioned the five young Canadians.

"Yeah," responded one of them. "You speak English?"

"Yes, of course," Pepito responded cheerfully. "What's up? What you say, bro? Let me holler at you."

The students burst out laughing.

"You are hilarious little man," stated the slender one with a rugged beard.

"You want to buy some snacks?" offered Pepito. "C'mon I got what you need. You need what I got... chips, crackers, cookies, nuts, I have it all, son." Pepito and Marta lifted the lids on their wicker boxes to reveal an assorted selection of small packaged snacks and treats.

This is what Pepito and Marta did most evenings - selling food items bought at the local store to foreigners at a 25 percent markup. Most of the tourists were either out for a stroll or waiting for the overnight buses that went to La Paz, Lima, or Arequippa. The snacks helped bring home some money for Pepito and Marta. They lived in the

Castro – one of Cusco's poorer neighbourhoods. It wasn't much, and some nights they would earn barely a sol or two, but every little bit helped. Pepito and Marta had been neighbours for most of their thirteen years. Both were only children, and as a result, grew up like siblings. Playing and arguing in equal measures.

"Do you have chocolate chip cookies?" asked the pretty brunette.

"I do," said Marta, "I have three packs."

"How much are they?"

"Three sols." The brunette reached into her jacket pocket and pulled out some coins.

"Here you go. Keep the change."

"Thanks. Do you guys want something else?" asked Marta.

"No thanks… we're good," offered the young couple that were huddled together.

"Come on, you don't want to get hungry…" enticed Pepito.

But before he had a chance to continue, Marta suddenly lunged forward letting out a strained grunt as though the air was being forced out of her lungs. The coins that were in her hand went flying through the air and bounced across the cobblestones on the ground. Pepito looked at Marta and realized she had been shoved from behind. Before he could process what he saw, he felt a firm grip on his wrist and then a sharp pain as his arm twisted behind his back. His breath was trapped in his throat. He wanted to yell, but couldn't. The attacker grabbed him by the sweater, and in an instant, Pepito was being pulled towards a car that was parked on the road nearby.

Overwhelmed with confusion, he looked over his shoulder. He couldn't see a face, just a black mask with holes cut out for the eyes and ears. Fear struck him like lightning bolt. "Who is this? What is happening?" He could barely make out Marta and the Canadians that seemed frozen with shock.

"H...h...help," Pepito managed to emit hoarsely; the knife-like pain still cutting into his shoulder.

"Hey!" "Wait!" "Come back here!" shouted the Canadians. Pepito could hear their footsteps and he hoped they were coming to his aid. Suddenly the car door swung open and Pepito was flung head first into the back seat. He fell into the well-worn upholstery as the attacker jumped into the back seat and slammed the car door behind him. Pepito looked through the window to his right to see Marta and the Canadians rushing towards the car. The masked man yelled out "Go! Let's go!" The driver stepped hard on the gas and the car squealed away from the curb. Pepito looked through the rear window as the bearded Canadian ran after the car, banging on the trunk with his fists. The driver accelerated and the car lunged forward and swerved into the traffic. A series of horns blared from the angry drivers cut off by the black sedan that darted its way between the two lanes of the thoroughfare.

Pepito's heart raced. He could feel it pounding in his chest. His breaths were short and hard, like pistons in an engine. He looked around. A round, burly figure was in the driver's seat. His leather jacket was ratty and a dragon tattoo peaked out above his neck collar. The driver was fixed on the road as he continued to weave through traffic, changing gears urgently. Pepito didn't dare to look his right, but he could feel the attacker still held a tight lock on his right wrist. Pepito looked down, in his periphery, he saw the man was wearing faded jeans and heavy, brown boots. The thug slid off his mask and shoved it into his jacket pocket. Pepito took several deep breaths, still rigid with fear. "Who are they? Why is this happening? What do they want?"

Suddenly the man in the front passenger's seat turned to reveal himself. He was young, in his early twenties. He had a scar that ran from his lower lip to his chin and his face was pock marked. His eyes were dark and unsympathetic. His upper lip curled up into a snarl as he examined Pepito,

"Relax, junior. Don't worry, everything is going to be alright." He had the sincerity of a snake oil salesman and the look of a stone-cold killer. His hair was jet black – slicked back with way too much hair gel. He also had a bluish green dragon tattoo crawling up his neck. "We're not going to hurt you. Unless you give us a reason to... just sit back and relax – we'll be there soon." He gave a wry smile, nodded his head twice, then turned away from Pepito and slumped into the front seat. Pepito could finally feel his breathing slow down and the drumming in his chest lessened. He looked through the window on his left. He recognized the storefronts; they were near the Castro, on the main road that cuts through the city.

The black sedan took a sudden left into one of the side streets. They continued for a few hundred metres, taking short turn after short turn, slicing through the web of narrow streets and alleyways. Then it dawned on Pepito, they were in El Campo: a neighbourhood just north of the Castro. This was gang territory. Its stories of violence were legendary. All the kids knew to stay away from El Campo. The only ones that came into this part of the city were the police and those looking for trouble. Pepito was neither one. His body stiffened again with fear.

The car slowed as it rounded into a narrow alley. There were boxes of garbage piled between a few darkened doorways. A metal garage door – barely wide enough for a car – slowly lifted and the sedan slid into an empty garage. The three car doors opened and the men stepped out. The scarred man came around to Pepito's side. He opened the door, grabbed his arm and led Pepito down a dingy hallway and into a room with a wooden table and a few ratted folding chairs. A single light bulb hung from the ceiling.

"Sit down," ordered the scarred face man.

Pepito hesitantly took a seat in the nearest chair. The man grabbed another chair from the far wall, flipped it around and sat within a couple of feet of Pepito. The man paused, collected his thoughts, and then glared intensely into Pepito's eyes.

"So… you are Jose Inti Capac, right? You live on 43 Calle Norte with your mother Rosita. Correct?" Pepito hated hearing his real name pronounced like that. It reminded him of how the nuns in Catechism school would address him. He felt a knot in his stomach – how dare this jerk mention his mother's name…

"You can talk now. Not cooperating would give me a reason to hurt you and I'm sure you wouldn't want that… your name is Jose Inti Capac - yes or no?" Pepito nodded. "Good. Good. That's all I need for now. Wait here, I'll be back." The scarred faced man stood up, turned and slipped into the room next door. Pepito could hear the three men talking through the thin drywall. He couldn't make out the words, just their muffled voices. He looked around the room, the walls were unfinished, not painted and held up in a makeshift manner. Pepito looked up to see an exposed ceiling. Metal beams ran across the tops of the walls. Perhaps they were in a warehouse or factory. The smell of burned oil hung in the air.

Pepito heard stories of gang members hiding out in such places. Offering the landlords protection in exchange for a safe place to hide from the police. Pepito's eyes darted across the room, it was empty except for the table and chairs and the few rags and crumpled papers that littered the concrete floor. Pepito grabbed the wooden table and slowly dragged it towards the wall, careful not to be heard by the thugs in the next room. He brought the chair across and used it as a stool to step onto the table. His hands slid up the drywall and he lifted his head to peer up and over the wall. There were a few inches between the beam and the wall and Pepito was able to steady himself to see down into the adjoining room. The three men were huddled around an office desk, their hands waving as they spoke to each other.

"Why wait, let's do it tonight," said the thug from the back seat.

"No, we need daylight in case he tries to run," retorted the scarred face man. "Let's wait until the morning. He's not going anywhere."

"The longer we wait, the more time the cops have of finding out."

"Don't worry about the cops – I told you they won't be a problem."

Pepito swallowed hard. "What do they want with him? What are they talking about?" Before he could further consider his own questions, his attention was drawn to the centre of the desk. His eyes narrowed as he focused on the objects between the three men. He couldn't believe what he saw. "Are those real? Is that what I think it is? Is that what this is about?" A flood of emotions swept over him. He was all at once confused, terrified and excited. His heart began racing again and his chest swelled. Sitting on a dilapidated desk in musty warehouse in the city's toughest neighbourhood was one of the greatest treasures in the history of the world.

# CHAPTER 2

**M**arta watched as the black sedan disappeared into the traffic ahead. She turned and ran back to where the baskets lay strewn on the ground. She thought for a moment, considered what to do next, then starting quickly across the parkette. She was so overcome with worry, that she ignored the Canadians and their pleas to help her and call the police. She didn't look back; she picked up her pace and before she knew it, she was in a full sprint down the sidewalk.

Marta ran down Calle Bolivar up to the bridge that crossed the highway and led into the Castro. She ran as fast as she could for the remaining six blocks. Her lungs burned, but she didn't stop until she reached the bottom of Calle Norte. The usual people were out in the street: some kids kicking a ball and a few older folks chatting on their stoops. She walked briskly until she reached Pepito's house.

She felt her hand shake as she knocked on the door. "Come on, come on," she thought. "Please be home." The door swung open and Pepito's mother greeted Marta with a warm smile.

"Ola Marta. How are you? Come in. Where's Pepito?"

The words rushed out of Marta like a fire hose. "He's gone. They took him! We were in the square and then they just came – they took him! This guy grabbed him and pulled him away into a car and they drove off. They just drove off with him!"

"Who? Who took him?" Rosita asked sharply.

"I don't know. He had a mask and I didn't see the guys in the car. I just saw the car drive off... It was black but I couldn't see anything else."

"Did they do anything to you? Did they rob you? Did they rob him?" Rosita's voice weighed with concern.

"No, they... he... just pushed me and grabbed Pepito's arm. He didn't even say anything. It happened so fast. They were gone before I knew what was happening."

Rosita took a long, deep breath. She held Marta's arms comfortingly. Her eyes darted back and forth as she processed the information. She then locked on Marta's eyes.

"Okay. Listen to me very carefully. You must not tell anyone about what happened. Do you understand? Not your parents, not the police, not your friends, not anyone. You need to keep quiet to protect yourself... Trust me. I know this doesn't make sense, but you need to act like nothing happened. Trust me, okay? In order to help Pepito you need to go home and stay there. Tomorrow, you do your normal routine and don't let on that anything is wrong."

"But we need to help him, we need to find Pepito," pleaded Marta.

"I know. I know... this... is...it's complicated. One day you will know more, but right now I need you to do what I ask. I beg you Marta, for Pepito's sake, please just go home and leave it with me." Rosita tried to muster a smile but her face was strained with pain and worry. Marta hesitated but she could tell by Rosita's tone that there was something bigger than her going on.

"Okay, but please tell me as soon as you find him. Tell me as soon as you know anything."

"I will, I will. I promise. Now go, okay?"

Marta turned and headed across the street. Rosita scanned the road from left to right. She looked to make sure Marta was safely inside. Rosita closed her door cautiously until she heard the click of the lock. She then dashed into the kitchen, she pulled open the bottom cupboard door and took out a red tablecloth. She darted up the two flights of stairs and went to the clothesline that spanned the rooftop terrace. Rosita fumbled in the metal bucket and pulled out three clothes pegs. She threw the red tablecloth on the line and secured it with the pegs. She looked across the rooftops. She prayed that the signal would be seen.

# CHAPTER 3

Every school kid in Peru knew the story of the Casa Del Oro – the House of Gold. The legend told of a house, or secret room, that housed the country's collection of priceless gold and jewels. The collection contained headdresses, masks, swords, shields, and other weapons that belonged to the Inca warriors and nobility in the days before the Spanish arrived. Before the 1500s, the Casa Del Oro was kept in Machu Picchu – the ancient Inca holy city, but it was believed to have been moved and hidden so that the Spanish conquistadors would never find it. Its location is a mystery and many a treasure hunter has sought to discover it. Everyone from rich foreigners to desperate outlaws have gone in search of the legendary riches. All have fallen short, losing both fortunes and lives along the way.

The legend also tells of an ancient map that reveals the location of the Casa Del Oro. The Circle Key – the Clave Circulo – is a stone, pie shaped circle made of four equal parts. When pieced together, its inscriptions and diagrams showed the way to the Casa's secret locale.

The Clave Circulo was Peru's national treasure, even though it too was lost and never seen in modern times. There was never a painting or drawing made of the Clave, its only details came from the retelling of the legend by the Inca elders. The Circle Key represented the power and mystery of the ancient Inca empire. Today it was a popular school time activity: kids would draw their own versions of the Clave and play out scavenger hunts in the school to search for an imaginary treasure.

Pepito believed it was just a fable, and if it did exist, the Circle Key was likely lost forever. He believed that until he saw those three pieces sitting on the table between the three thugs.

"Okay, we'll wait until morning," said the driver to the scarred face man. "You're the boss." The driver then took out a canvas bag from the desk drawer and placed the three pieces inside the bag.

"No sense leaving it out in the open," he said as he carefully placed the bag back into the drawer.

"You need to get some food for the kid," ordered the scarred face man. "Some water and a sandwich or something. We need him healthy. Go to the store on the corner. Tell them to put it on my tab."

The driver strode out of the room and down

the hallway opposite the garage. A door creaked open in the distance.

Pepito furrowed his brow. "What did they want with him?" He still had no idea why he was taken and brought there.

Suddenly there was a loud rapping on the metal garage door.

"Open up," said a raspy voice. "It's Castillo."

The scarred faced man and the driver headed out of the room. Pepito jumped down from the table and quickly went for the chair. The two men passed by in the hallway just as he fell into the chair's cheap plastic. Pepito heard the men open the garage door and a third man entered.

"So, what happened?" asked the scarred face man.

"Just like we thought. The gringos in the park called the police, they came, took down their information and then left. They got nothing," said the stranger.

"And the girl?"

"She ran off. Cruz tried following her but she gave him the slip. We think she went home. By the time he got to her house, she wasn't around. Probably scared and hiding under her bed..."

The stranger chuckled menacingly.

"This is it," thought Pepito. "This is my chance." Pepito was notoriously impulsive. He was forever being scolded by his mother for not thinking before he acted. "I have to go now. It's now or never." Pepito slinked out of the chair and into the hallway. He paused. He could hear the thugs' voices but they were hidden from view in the garage. He looked to his right at the desk in the adjacent room. He let out a short breath.

"Do it," he thought.

Pepito snuck into the room and approached the desk. He slowly opened the drawer and lifted the canvas bag. He slung it over his shoulder. The stones were lighter than he expected. He cautiously approached the hallway. The men were still talking in the garage. He turned to his right and made his way down the hallway. He passed other sparsely furnished rooms. Inside he could see stained couches, old computers, and television sets. His heart was racing. He could see the glass door ahead. Forty feet away. His legs moved swiftly, barely touching the floor. Thirty feet. He was nearly there. Twenty feet. He could see the streetlights outside. Ten feet. He reached for the door...

"Hey! Get back here!" yelled out the scarred face man. "Don't take another step!"

The hair stood up on the back of Pepito's neck. He didn't turn around. He kept moving forward. He pushed hard on the door and it swung open violently. The streetlamps made small puddles of light on the sidewalk. Pepito jumped from the doorway and onto the sidewalk. He could hear the footsteps of the men rushing towards him. His eyes darted up and down the street. The stores were closed and the street was nearly vacant; Pepito could make out the dark shadows of some people off in the distance. He turned and ran towards them. In an instant, Pepito was running at full stride, his arms and legs slicing through the night air. The bag bounced off his hip, Pepito swung it behind his back and kept darting ahead. He couldn't hear the men behind him – he couldn't hear anything at all, except for his quick, harsh breaths. Pepito raced towards the people – he could see now that they were two men standing in front of a restaurant, a cigarette dangling from each of their hands.

Pepito approached them, his adrenalin was still firing and he had to force his legs to slow down.

"Hey...hey...I'm being...help... I need your help..." Pepito barely managed to get the words out between gasps. "Those guys are after me... they are trying to get me."

"Who? Who's after you?" asked the heavy-set man with a round face.

"Those guys." Pepito turned around and pointed. The three thugs had stopped running and were walking briskly towards Pepito and the two strangers. "They kidnapped me," blurted out. The two strangers were struck by his words.

"They kidnapped you? Why?" said the other man. Pepito turned back to see the thugs had stopped and were now walking back huddled, trying to conceal themselves.

"I don't know," responded Pepito. "But can you please help me? Can you help me to get home?"

"Uh...yeah... okay, sure," said the heavy-set man. He could see the panic and fear in Pepito's eyes. "Where do you live? I can give you ride if you want."

"Not too far, in the Castro."

"Okay. My car is right here – I can take you now, let's go." The sympathetic stranger rubbed out his cigarette with his shoe and pulled his keys from his pocket. Pepito and the man climbed into the car, Pepito gave him directions to his house, and they headed down the road.

"I have to get home," he thought. "I have to see my mother." Pepito had lived his entire life with Rosita. The only constant they ever had in life was each other. Their bond was forged by enduring years of hardship. They were each other's everything. Pepito thought of what he would say once he saw Rosita. He thought of what she might think or say. Then he suddenly remembered something Rosita said to him when he was about six or seven years old. It hit him like a slap to the face.

"Wait," he said. "We can't go to my house. There is another place you have to take me..."

# CHAPTER 4

Pepito recalled the day seven years ago when Rosita sat him down at the kitchen table and knelt down in front of him.

"Pepito. I need to tell you something very important, okay? Don't be afraid, my love. But you need to know this. Don't be scared, okay? If something happens to you...if you feel unsafe for any reason... then you need to go a special place. Do you know Senhor Osuna's house? The house with the yard behind the back alley? There is a big shed in the corner of the yard. If you ever feel scared then I want you to go to the shed, okay? You will find a key under a rock beside the door. If anything ever happens you go there. Do you understand?"

Pepito was worried that day sitting in the kitchen. His mother had never said anything to cause him any concern before that or ever since. Life had been fairly routine and typical. He was just another poor kid growing up in Cusco. He didn't think his life or anyone he knew was special or unique. That was what he thought until that creep grabbed him in the square.

The kind stranger's car pulled up to Senhor Osuna's house. Pepito thanked the man and ambled out of the passenger's seat. He made his way down the narrow passage between the two houses and approached the metal gate that led to backyard. He could see the shed in the distant corner of the yard. A small, single bulb above the door lit the grass and dirt that surrounded the shed. Pepito unlatched the gate and headed for the shed. He was about to knock gently, but before he could, the door swung open. Pepito took a step back. He could only make out the shadow of the person in the doorway. His eyes adjusted to the light and he was able to make out the soft, delicate face of his mother. Rosita stood there welcoming him with outstretched arms.

"Come here, my love."

Pepito moved towards her and fell into her arms. He held her tightly. All the fear he had restrained earlier came flooding forward and Rosita could feel his body shaking.

"It's okay, baby... it's okay... Don't worry, you're safe now..." Rosita said comfortingly. She stroked the back of his head and softly kissed his temple. "Everything is fine now. No one is going to hurt you..."

Pepito could feel his arms go limp. For the

first time since the abduction he was able to relax. He took a deep breath as a wave of fatigue swept over him. "Mama..." He started. "Mama, I need to tell you what happened..."

"Come, my love. Come in here." Rosita turned towards the inside of the shed. For the first time, Pepito looked around. He was taken aback by what he saw. On one side, there were two small cots with pillows and blankets laid on top. In the other corner, there was a compact kitchen with a counter top, sink, and single burner stove. Rosita sat down on one of the lumpy mattresses and motioned for Pepito to do the same. He continued to scan the shed. Pepito saw three closet doors with locks on the handles. He scrunched his face. "What is this place? Is this a shed? Someone's house?"

"Just sit down and tell me everything," said Rosita soothingly.

Pepito sat down on the cot facing his mother. He could feel the weariness in his legs. He thought for a moment. The evening's events flashed across his mind like scenes from a movie. When he was finally able to collect himself, he began recounting everything that happened. Rosita listened intently; her eyes were locked on Pepito as he spoke. Rosita appeared concerned and troubled by his words, but strangely, she did not seem surprised.

When Pepito finished, Rosita took a long, deep breath and exhaled slowly.

"Show me the Clave Circulo, Pepito," she

said with trepidation.

Pepito swung the bag around and pulled out the three stone pieces. Rosita took one and examined it closely. Her fingers slid over the carvings of a sun and a mountain. Just as she had feared: it was authentic. She closed her eyes and thought pensively for a moment. The day she had feared for nearly fourteen years was here. She had to be strong.

Rosita lifted her head, "Pepito. These are real. This is the real Clave Circulo. This is incredibly valuable and we need to make sure that it doesn't fall into the wrong hands. We need to get this back to where it belongs."

"Why don't we call the police? Tell them about the thugs and give the Clave Circulo to the police?"

"We can't. We must return this to a very specific place and to some very specific people. This may be confusing right now and I promise you will learn more, but right now, we need to get this back safely."

"I don't get it," said Pepito shaking his head.

"Tomorrow you will go to a building downtown on Calle Principle. It is a safe house. The men there will protect the Clave. They are a special kind of police and they will know what to do...do you remember St. Anthony's Church near Plaza Inti?"

Pepito nodded.

"Across the street there is a narrow building

with brown stucco and a black doorway with no windows. There is a small buzzer to the right of the door. Press the buzzer three times. A voice will come on the intercom. Tell them you are there to buy a black sampona (samponas were a native Peruvian instrument and were always beige or cream colored – never black). Say it just like that, 'I want to buy a black sampona'. The men will let you in and take care of everything. You will be safe there."

"Why can't we go together? Why don't you come with me?"

Rosita paused. She was torn with indecision. Her heart ached. Her son had been through so much and now she was leaving him on his own again.

"I have to stay here. I have to protect this place."

Pepito's head was swirling. He had so many questions. He looked at his mother.

"I know," she said, "you're confused. But after tomorrow things will make more sense. Don't be worried. Don't be scared."

Rosita tried to convince Pepito that he was no longer in danger, but what she didn't realize was that his troubles had only just begun.

# CHAPTER 5

MARCH 19<sup>TH</sup>, 7:55am

Pepito lifted his eyes. The morning light seeped in through the cracks in the shed. Pepito strained to focus on his surroundings. He sighed. It was real, not a dream. He sat up in the cot and looked around. Rosita was standing over the miniature sink.

"Good morning, sweetie," she said.

"Good morning," responded Pepito groggily.

"How did you sleep? Are you hungry?"

Pepito nodded.

"I'll go to the house to make some breakfast...but... first, I want to tell you something." Rosita bent down and pulled a brown wooden box out from the cupboard below the sink. She sat on the cot next to him. "I had trouble sleeping last night – worried that you were frightened. You have to understand why I need to stay here and send you on your own." Rosita pulled the box onto her lap. "I wasn't going to show you this... but I think you need to know..."

Rosita pulled the small brass latch and lifted the lid on the box. Pepito looked inside. He let out a slight gasp. Sitting in the box, nestled in straw, was the fourth piece of the Clave Circulo.

Pepito stumbled to find the right words, "But... what... why do you have this?"

"It's a very long story and one that will be revealed to you soon, I promise." Rosita hated keeping anything from Pepito but right now getting him to safety was her first priority.

"Did you steal this? Is that why the thugs are after me?" asked Pepito.

"I didn't steal anything. Those men are after this and it is very important that they don't ever get their hands on it. It's complicated, my love. Just trust me for now, okay?" Rosita stood up. "We need to get going...wash up and get dressed... I'll go make some eggs, I'll be back soon." Rosita opened the shed door and made her way towards the rear entrance of Senhor Osuna's house.

Pepito followed his mother's orders. He put on his clothes and used the sink to brush his teeth and wash his face. Thoughts and questions ricocheted through his head. He tried to calm down but he was gripped with fear and uncertainty. "How did the key get here?" he thought. "How is my mother connected to all this? What and who is at that safe house?"

Pepito decided to step into the yard to get some fresh air. Pepito looked around, surveying the familiar surroundings. He took a few steps toward the wire fence that separated the property from the rear laneway. Pepito recalled how often he and his friends had run down this very spot kicking a soccer ball or playing hide and seek. All those years of blind innocence, completely unaware that a precious treasure lay only a few metres away.

Pepito's thoughts were interrupted by the sound of a car passing by on the street. He heard the car slow down and then the grinding of gears as it was placed in reverse. The car was heading back towards the front of the house. Just as it passed between the houses, Pepito could see the unmistakable outline of the thugs' black sedan.

"Oh no," he thought, "They're here!" Pepito darted back into the shed, he scrambled under the cot and pulled up the canvas bag. He looked at the wooden box on the adjacent bed. There was no time to think - he grabbed the fourth piece of the Circulo, placed it in the bag, and then swung it over his shoulder. He rushed out of the shed, shut the door, and scrambled behind the shed. His heart was pounding. Rosita was still inside. He poked his head around the shed to see if he could spot her in one of the windows. "What should I do? Should I warn her? Try and get inside? What about protecting the Circulo?" His mind raced at lightning speed.

Before he had a chance to make up his mind, he spotted the scarred face man sneaking slowly towards the gate between the houses.

The man carefully lifted the latch and slinked into the rear yard, staying close to the house. Pepito's chest thundered. "What should I do?" He clenched his teeth and gripped the bag tightly. He watched as the man peeked into the basement window, cupping his face to get a look inside. The man then reached up with both hands and grabbed the bottom ledge of the first-floor window. He pulled himself up and peered inside.

Pepito knew this was his best shot to escape. He quietly stepped backwards, turned, and carefully hopped over the three-foot metal fence. He could hear the fence creaking under foot and he prayed the scarred face man was too far to hear anything. He jumped and landed on the laneway with a light thud. He looked back towards the house, but the shed blocked his view. Pepito stood for a moment, unsure if he should leave his mother behind. He wanted desperately to help her, but he knew he couldn't do it alone. He wondered what she would say to him right now. With that in mind, Pepito clutched the canvas bag and started running down the laneway.

# CHAPTER 6

The cars whirred by as Pepito stood a half block from St. Anthony's church. He knew the church well; he was baptized here and his Confirmation ceremony took place only a few weeks earlier. He recalled how proud he felt that day in his new navy suit and black patent leather shoes. The shoes were a bit tight but he joked that they helped him stay awake during the long mass. He thought about his friends and how excited they were in their new duds. Even Marta dressed up for the occasion, she wore a pretty yellow dress instead of her usual track pants and hoodie. Pepito had always seen Marta in a ponytail and he was taken aback when she walked into the church with her shiny brown hair sitting softly around her shoulders.

A car horn blared, snapping Pepito back into the reality of the moment. The street was a busy cluster of cars and pedestrians. He looked across the street and scanned the buildings beside the church. He recognized the small housewares store on the north side, but he had never noticed the narrow doorway with the windowless brown door beside it. The door blended seamlessly into the building's façade. There were no numbers or names visible, only a large, round brass handle in the middle. Pepito took a few steps along the sidewalk in the direction of the church. He could make out the doorbell buzzer set within the doorway's inner wall.

Pepito stopped. Something didn't feel right. He felt nervous and uneasy. He examined the people as they went by; unfamiliar faces out shopping on a typical Saturday. He heard the sounds of street vendors hawking their wares and pan flute music coming from the market off in the distance. Pepito glanced to his left, at the Mirador Hotel – a young foreigner with a backpack entered the front entrance; he looked tired and in need of some rest and a good meal.

Pepito looked to his right. He gazed at the café on the corner. The café's large glass windows overlooked Calle Principal and the cross street, Avenida Bolivar. Pepito leaned towards the café and craned his neck to get a look inside the front window. A young family sat at the table nearest the door – pastries and drinks rested on their table. Pepito looked behind them. He gasped. Standing behind a pillar in the far corner of the café was the driver thug. The driver tried to look inconspicuous but Pepito could see him glancing nervously at the people strolling by.

Pepito turned and began to walk briskly down the sidewalk away from the café. He turned left at the first intersection and ducked into a small courtyard that marked the entrance to a series of low rise apartments. Pepito stood behind a row of shrubs and exhaled deeply. "The thugs know everything," he thought. "They know where I live, where I'm going, everything..." Pepito considered where to go next. The thugs obviously knew about the safe houses and where he lived. His family wasn't safe and neither was he. "Think...just calm down and think..." Pepito thought about all the people in his life that the thugs could get to. He was angry and frustrated that those creeps had put him and his family in such peril. He couldn't bear the idea of something terrible happening to the people he loved.

And then it dawned on him, "There is one person that can help... I just hope he's home." With renewed optimism, Pepito hurried out of the courtyard and scrambled his way up the steep cobblestoned street to the San Blas neighbourhood.

# CHAPTER 7

Senhor Gonzalez's cheerful face was framed by his salt and pepper hair and short beard. He smiled easily and his eyes twinkled; particularly when he was talking about Peruvian history to his students. Pepito loved Social Studies class, partly because he was fascinated with the subject matter, and partly because Senhor Gonzalez had a way of bringing the class to life.

Senhor Gonzalez was pleasantly surprised to see Pepito standing at his door.

"Pepito! Hello, how are you? Come in, come in..." Senhor Gonzalez noticed the look of concern on Pepito's face. "Is everything okay, Pepito?"

"I'm sorry to bother you. I need your help. Do you think I can use your phone? I need to call... make sure my...I need to call home."

"Yes, of course. Come on in. You can use the phone in here."

Senhor Gonzalez recognized that Pepito was not his usual cheerful self. He hoped that everything was alright as he led Pepito into the living room.

The home was modest yet tastefully decorated. Native Peruvian art pieces hung on the walls and the room was filled with stocked bookshelves.

"The phone is on the table by the couch," pointed Senhor Gonzalez. "I'll get us a snack. I'll be back."

Pepito sat on the corner of the aged leather sofa and dialed a number that he had dialed hundreds of times before. It started to ring. "Please pick up...please pick up..."

"Hello?"

Pepito had never been so happy to hear that warm, familiar voice.

"Marta? It's Pepito."

"Pepito! Where are you? Are you okay?"

"Yeah, I'm okay. I'm at Senhor Gonzalez's house. I'm safe now."

"What happened? Who were those guys? Where did they take you?"

"They took me to some building in El Campo but I got away from them. Listen...I need you to do me a favour," Pepito said directly. "I need you to go to Senhor Osuna's house. You know, the house behind the back alley?"

"Yeah, I know," Marta responded, "the one with the big back yard."

"My mom is there. I need you to go to the house and make sure she is fine. Can you do that?

Call me right back at this number. I need you to go right now, okay?"

Marta could hear the concern in his voice. She was worried for Pepito and his mom. They are like family and she felt sick knowing they were in danger.

"Yeah, of course. I'll go right now. I'll call you back as soon as I can."

"Okay, thanks. Marta... make sure that..." He struggled to find the right words, "just make sure that you stay safe, okay?"

"I will," Marta responded softly.

Pepito put the phone back on the cradle and let out a deep, nervous sigh. His foot tapped anxiously against the hardwood floor and he could feel his palms getting moist with sweat. He could hear Senhor Gonzalez making his way down the hall. He entered the living room carrying a tray with glasses of juice and a plate of picarones. Senhor Gonzalez set the tray down on the large ottoman and invited Pepito to help himself. Pepito hadn't realized how hungry he was as he devoured the first pastry in a single bite. He apologized for his lack of manners in between large gulps of juice.

"It's quite alright," said Senhor Gonzalez reassuringly. "No need to be sorry about being hungry... So, tell me Pepito, what brought you here? Is something going on?" Senhor Gonzalez glanced down at the bag sitting on Pepito's lap.

"Well, no. Things are fine. I just needed..."

Pepito didn't feel comfortable keeping the truth from his teacher, but he didn't want to implicate him in a situation that was still a mystery to Pepito. "I came here to ask you...to get some information."

"What kind of information?" asked Senhor Gonzalez.

"Do you remember when you told us about the Clave Circulo?"

"Yes, of course I do."

"I was hoping you could tell me more about it. The details and stuff. I remember what you told us in class, but maybe you could tell me what the images on the map mean."

Senhor Gonzalez was not sure what to make of Pepito's inquiry, but he responded nonetheless.

"Well, like I explained in class, the Circulo is a key and when placed together, the four pieces display a map. The common theory is that the map shows a specific place or altar in Machu Picchu where the key is to be placed. During the spring equinox – the most sacred day in the Inca calendar – the sun's light will pass through the centre of the key and point you in the direction of the treasure; the Casa Del Oro. Supposedly the light casts a shadow of a snake and the snake's mouth points the way to the entrance to the Casa. People also theorize that the pieces themselves are the keys to enter the building. Of course, there is also -" Senhor Gonzalez's explanation was cut short by the sudden ringing of the phone on the side table. "Hold on, Pepito." Senhor Gonzalez reached over and picked up the phone. "Hello? Yes...yes, he is here. Sure, just a moment." He passed the phone towards Pepito, "It's for you."

"Hello?" answered Pepito, his voice shaking ever so slightly.

"Pepito, it's Marta. I went as quickly as I could to Senhor Osuna's house."

"And what happened? Did you talk to my mother?"

"No, she wasn't there. I talked to Senhor Osuna. He said your mom is okay – she is not in danger. He wants you to know that she left with an old friend and that they are both safe. He said there's no reason for you to worry and that you should stay where you are. They will try and find you."

A series of clicks sounded through the phone.

"Marta, are you still there?" asked Pepito.

"Yeah. What was that noise?"

"I don't know...did he say anything else?"

"No, just what I told you...make sure you take care of yourself, okay? I don't want you to get hurt." Pepito was comforted by Marta's concern.

"Don't worry, I'll be okay. I'll talk to you soon...oh hey, Marta..."

"Yeah?"

"Thanks."

"No problem. Talk to you soon."

"Okay..." Pepito hung up the phone and

passed it back to Senhor Gonzalez.

"Is everything alright?" he asked.

"Yes everything is just fine..." Pepito answered. Senhor Gonzalez could see he was being guarded. "Don't worry about it. Please continue with the story – what were you saying? There is something else about the key?" Senhor Gonzalez hesitated to continue. He worried about Pepito's nervous demeanor. He didn't want to upset Pepito so he tried to act naturally and continued with the explanation.

"Historians believe that the treasure has been moved, maybe more than once. The Casa's whereabouts are unknown so it's possible that it has been relocated to keep the thieves guessing. The Circulo is the starting point but the end point remains a mystery to us all...wait a minute...today, today is the $19^{th}$, it's the $19^{th}$ of March."

"Yes, I think so. Why?"

"The equinox is tomorrow. I hadn't realized it, but tomorrow is the day that the Circulo can be used to reveal the Casa's location." Pepito was suddenly struck by his teacher's words. That's why the thugs were after him and in a hurry to collect the pieces. They knew this moment only comes about once a year.

"Senhor Gonzalez, do you believe the Casa del Oro exists?" asked Pepito. "Do you think it's real?" Senhor Gonzalez took a deep breath and contemplated the question.

"Well... I do. I understand that legends make great stories and I know the search has been a fruitless one for over 500 years, but our people have a history woven with acts of bravery, strength, and sophistication. I have an intuitive sense that the legend of the Casa and its whereabouts is based ... The order of events and the pieces of the story might be muddled, but I can't help but think our Incan ancestors have the answer and are smiling down on us from the heavens." Pepito tightened his grip on the canvas bad and a small grin curled in the corner of his mouth. For the first time in two days he felt excited about his predicament. He was in the middle of an historic incident and he had the power to decide how the story would unfold. The fate of the Circulo's secret rested quite literally in the palm of his hand and he felt that it was his destiny to see it through to the end.

Suddenly Pepito remembered the clicking sound he heard on the telephone. He wondered what could have caused that. Maybe the conversation was being recorded, or maybe it was the thugs listening in. "That's crazy," he thought. "Only in the movies do they listen in on personal phone lines." But the last few days had felt like a movie – a thrilling yet dangerous one at that. Pepito could not take a chance. If the thugs were listening, then Senhor Gonzalez' place was no longer safe. For his and his teacher's safety, Pepito needed to get out of there.

"Senhor Gonzalez. I really appreciate you taking the time to help me and I thank you for the food... very kind of you. I need to get going, I... just want to thank you again." Pepito stood up from the couch.

"You're quite welcome – anytime." Senhor Gonzalez stood up, reached into his pocket, and pulled out his wallet. "Here, take this." He handed Pepito two 50 soles notes. "In case you want to buy more picarones on your way home." He gave Pepito a wink and the two made their way to the front foyer. "Please say hello to your mother for me."

"I will," said Pepito.

Senhor Gonzalez placed a hand on Pepito's shoulder as he approached the door.

"Remember Pepito if you need anything or if you need to tell me something – don't hesitate. You can trust me." Pepito nodded and extended his hand.

"Thank you again, Senhor Gonzalez. I'll see you on Monday." Pepito shook Senhor Gonzalez' hand, turned to open the door, and then walked out into the bright sunlight. Senhor Gonzalez watched as Pepito turned down the narrow cobblestone street that led back down into Cusco's lower, downtown district.

Pepito walked cautiously down the winding road. He felt exposed as he walked past the neatly kept homes with the tidy window boxes-filled with blooming flowers. Pepito's head swiveled as he looked around. The street was quiet except for the distant sound of children playing at the nearby park. Pepito kept walking down toward the centre of town. He approached the small park that sat on the corner between Calle Verdun and Avenida Mirador. Pepito could see about a half dozen children chasing each other around the metal climbing structure in the middle of the large sand box. He picked up his pace and crossed the street into the park. Pepito spotted a bench where two women sat. There was an empty seat at the end of the bench; he slinked over and sat down. From this vantage point he could see the roads while the young mothers blocked him from view.

Pepito sat and pondered what to do next. "Where could I go? Where would I be safe now?" Several minutes passed as Pepito replayed the details of his conversation with Senhor Gonzalez. He recalled seeing the passion in his teacher's eyes. The Circulo epitomizes the hopes and history of the Peruvian people. Pepito was so absorbed in his own thoughts that he failed to see the black sedan slowly driving towards him.

# CHAPTER 8

**M**arta hung up the phone with Pepito and looked vacantly around the kitchen. She was worried that he was involved in something dangerous and that he was in over his head. "What did those thugs want?" she thought. "Why is Pepito at Senhor Gonzalez' house?" Nothing seemed to make sense to her and she felt frustrated and powerless. Marta sat for several minutes, questions swirling in her head. "Where is Rosita? Why did Pepito send her to Senhor Osuna's house?" So many questions and she couldn't come up with any reasonable answers.

Marta finally decided to make her way to Pepito's house. She stepped outside and walked across the street. She rapped lightly on the heavy wooden door. The street was quiet today. Usually, there were kids playing soccer outside and the odd adult sweeping the stoop or chatting with other neighbours. But today for some reason, everyone had stayed inside. Marta knocked again.

She leaned in towards the window and cupped her hands in front of her face. Her eyes adjusted to the glare from the glass and she was able to make out the entranceway in Pepito's house. The lights were off and there was no movement inside. Again, things seemed oddly quiet.

Marta took a step back and looked up at the second-floor window. She thought about how in the summer, when the window was open, she would call out to Pepito and invite him out to play. That window was the pipeline of their relationship. But today it was shut and closed off – much like the way she felt about Pepito and the situation he was in. Marta sighed and decided to walk back to her house. As she turned, she caught sight of something in the distance at the end of the road. Sitting parked by the curb at the far end of the street was a dark coloured car. She hadn't noticed it before – maybe it was there when she crossed the street, but there it sat now, parked in isolation.

Marta tried to act naturally as she crossed the street. She gave a few quick glances down the road to get a better look at the car. It looked like a black car, maybe the same one that kidnapped Pepito, but she wasn't sure. She took the last few steps across the sidewalk and reached for her door. Just as she grabbed the doorknob, she heard a sharp squeal from down the road. She spun her head to see the car dart from the curb and lurch its way up the street towards her. The engine roared as the car gathered speed and began hurt-ling closer and closer. Marta turned the doorknob as quickly as she could, flung the door open and dashed inside. Just as she turned to close the door, the black sedan roared past her. It was a blur going by, but she was able to make out two young, dark haired men in the car – they looked different from the men in the square and even the car didn't look like the same as the kidnapper's – this one was older and even more beat up. She slammed the door closed, quickly turned the dead bolt and then fell against the door. The car continued to speed past the house and down the road. Marta's heart raced and adrenalin pumped through her veins. "Oh my god," she thought, "Oh my god..."

# CHAPTER 9

Pepito shifted in his seat to block himself from the thugs' view. The young mothers sitting beside him continued to chat idly, completely unaware of the situation happening around them. The black sedan slowly drove towards the park. Pepito sat perfectly still. He could no longer see the car as it approached – he dared not to move for fear of being seen. The black sedan continued its slow pace and rolled passed the park and the children playing innocently on the climbing structure.

Several seconds passed. Pepito tilted his head back slightly and caught a glimpse of the car as it approached the intersection of Calle Verdun and Avenida Mirador. The car came to a complete stop. The tinted windows prevented Pepito from seeing who was in the car, but he become increasingly worried as the car remained stationary. The intersection was about 80 metres away. Pepito thought that if the car went into reverse, he would dart across the park behind him and into the busy plaza that led into the adjacent neighbourhood. He waited. Several more seconds passed and still the car did not move.

"They must know I'm here. They must have seen me," thought Pepito. He grabbed the bag with both hands, ready to make a break for it. He took a deep breath, leaned forward to get up, and then he stopped. The black sedan began rolling. It turned left and proceeded slowly up Calle Verdum and began ascending the road that led back to San Blas and Senhor Gonzalez' place. He watched carefully as the car travelled up the road and out of view. Pepito exhaled. For the first time, the women took notice of Pepito and glanced at him. He smiled, suddenly filled with relief. He was right about the thugs and his conversation with Marta. They were listening and they were aware of his previous location. He didn't have much time before they would realize he was no longer at Senhor Gonzalez's house. He needed to keep moving. Pepito stood up and began crossing the park towards Avenida Mirador. He reached the sidewalk and started quickly down the street. He knew Terminal Terrestre wasn't far, maybe twenty minutes if he didn't stop or slow down. Pepito kept moving, occasionally glancing over his shoulder. He wasn't very familiar with this area of town, but he knew if he continued downward he would make his way to Avenida Central and Cusco's main bus terminal.

◆ ◆ ◆

Saturdays were always busy at the bus terminal. Young families, older peasants from the countryside, and a few tourists all shuffled about the ticket windows and the numerous bus stops surrounding the blue and white building. Pepito veered through the crowd and approached the last ticket window – he preferred to stay out of sight as much as possible. He looked around as he waited in line. So many people were innocently going about their lives, coming and going without realizing the secret Pepito possessed in his bag. Pepito chuckled to himself thinking, "If they only knew...".

The ticket agent called out to him, "Next, please." Pepito stepped towards the window. He reached into his pocket and pulled out one of the 50 sol notes.

"One ticket to Ollantaytambo, please," he said, sliding the note on the counter.

"Eight sols," replied the agent. "Go to bus stand number six. It's at the back of the building. The bus leaves in about 15 minutes."

"Thank you," said Pepito as he took the change and ticket off the counter. Pepito turned back towards the crowd. "Am I doing the right thing?" he thought. Maybe it wasn't the right thing to do, but he felt compelled to keep going, his journey had brought him this far and he truly felt this was his destiny. No time to worry about that right now, it was time to find something to drink and bus stop number six.

The bus driver turned the key and the bus chugged to life. The bus was half filled with a myriad of people. An elderly couple sat across from Pepito. The harsh lines on their faces a result of the many years toiling in the fields, exposed to wind and sun. They both sat solemnly and stared straight ahead. Pepito couldn't help but feel sorry for them, they've had a hard life and daily survival is likely an unrelenting reality for them. Pepito respected the sacrifices and hard work demonstrated by the farmers living in the countryside. He knew the *campesinos'* efforts fed the country and their place in society was greatly underappreciated. Perhaps sensing Pepito's stare, the older lady turned and looked at Pepito. Her eyes were dark round pools, set deeply behind her wrinkled skin, but they exuded a gentle warmth. He offered her a slight smile. She examined Pepito – glanced down at his bag and then gave him what looked like a knowing smile. She nodded slightly and then turned her head and continued to look out the front window. Pepito was beguiled by the old lady. He couldn't help but think that she knew the contents of the bag and that she was along for the adventure. Perhaps his last two days had made him paranoid and wary of everyone around him. "Just relax," he told himself, "no one knows you and no one knows you're here."

The bus laboured along the winding roads that connected Cusco with the Sacred Valley. The surrounding mountains were a constant shift of brown and green hues. Fields of corn, beets, and potatoes filled the gaps between the Vilconata River and the steep faces of the mountainsides. Pepito watched as the afternoon sun danced playfully on the undulating mountains; he was struck by the beauty of the countryside. The Sacred Valley formed the heart of the Incan Empire and even though it sat a short drive from Cusco, it seemed timeless and Pepito felt a strong connection to his ancestors that once lived and thrived in the area.

Pepito's thoughts drifted. He wondered how his mother was doing. Was she thinking of him, too? He wished there was a way he could communicate with her and let her know that he was safe. He knew somehow that his mother would support his choice to follow the Circulo. Throughout his childhood, his mother preached independence and self-reliance. "Don't ask others to do what you can do yourself," was another of her common expressions.

The bus suddenly slowed and veered to the side of the road. They had arrived in Urubamba, an ancient town nestled along the river.

The bus stop was located at the edge of the town's limits and there was a small cluster of people waiting. Several passengers disembarked from the bus. Pepito watched as a young family with a couple of suitcases slid along the aisle and out the front door. Then two men boarded the bus. They were in their early twenties and dressed in black. They stood out to Pepito, because unlike the other passengers, they carried nothing with them – no bags, backpacks, no possessions whatsoever.

Pepito felt unnerved as they walked past him in the aisle and took a seat at the back of the bus. Pepito glanced over his shoulder. The two men were seated close together and spoke in inaudible whispers. He shivered with fear. "What if they were with the thugs? What if they knew what was in the bag?"

The bus surged forward and began to ramble down the highway once again. Pepito tried to allay his fears. His destination, Ollantaytambo, was less than 30 minutes away. He just needed to remain calm until then. He took a long, deep breath. They were likely two friends traveling together and completely oblivious to his situation. Perhaps he had nothing to fear but his own paranoia.

He decided to try and appear natural and occupy his thoughts with anything other than the two men behind him. Pepito thought of Marta and how he wished she was with him. Other than his mother, Marta was the toughest person he knew.

Since they were kids he was impressed with how she handled herself with the other boys. School breaks always meant playing soccer in the yard and Marta was always in goal taking on the bigger, and often older, kids. Scraped knees and a fiery disposition – that was Marta. Taunting the boys to kick the ball harder, "Come on you wimps! Let me see what you got!" She would holler at them. Pepito couldn't help but smile thinking about those endless games in the yard, Marta's lively eyes, and the image of her with her small hands wrapped fiercely around the tattered ball. Marta was more protective of more than just the soccer net. On more than a few occasions she came to Pepito's defence when the group of mean kids teased him about his father.

"I hear your dad is in jail," they would begin. "Maybe he made the licence plate on my car." The other students would burst out laughing or others would simply walk past relieved that they weren't the source of the boys' verbal abuse. But Marta wouldn't stand for it. She would stride over to them, point her finger in their faces and say, "Why don't you grow up and show some respect? You should be ashamed of picking on him for something he had nothing to do with." Marta's scolding was often enough for the mean kids to back off Pepito and leave him alone.

Marta never directly asked Pepito about his father. Like the others, she heard rumours that he went to prison shortly after Pepito was born.

The speculation among the school kids ranged from armed robbery to attempted murder. Marta knew the topic was a painful one for Pepito and she never wanted to cause him any undue pain, so she never brought it up. It was a private family matter and no one had the right to disrespect Pepito for events that happened when he was an infant. Marta felt it was her duty to protect Pepito from the insensitivities of others, and if that meant standing toe to toe with some jerks, then so be it.

The sound of the gears grinding awoke Pepito from his day dream. He looked through the bus's windshield and saw that they were nearing the town. Ollantaytambo was once in the heart of the Sacred Valley and its hillsides are strewn with the ruins of ancient Incan dwellings. The new town was built among and between towering stone structures and rock walls that formed flat terraces. Pepito wondered how the Incas were able to carve and assemble such massive pieces of stone without machines and modern tools. The stones that were used to build the structures were laid with such precision and accuracy. Pepito once again swelled with pride for his people and the majesty of their historical achievements.

The bus once again veered from the main

road and pulled into the side street that led to the town's bus station. There was a busy hive of activity as people shuffled around the town's central shopping area. The smell of fresh produce filled the air. Pepito watched as two campisanos held an animated conversation over a stall of beets and potatoes. Arms waving in the air; they were no doubt arguing over price.

The brakes let out a high pitch screech as the bus rolled to a stop. The passengers on the bus stood up and collected their belongings. Pepito slung the bag over his shoulder and began down the aisle towards the front of the bus. He turned to look behind him. The two young men had also started to make their way towards the exit as they moved swiftly from their seats.

Pepito felt uneasy; he rushed out of the bus and darted through the crowd of people assembled outside. He tried to stay calm as he passed through the bus terminal parking lot back to the side street that connected to the rest of the town's core. He slid around the corner and ducked into a souvenir shop. While hiding behind a rack of soccer shirts, he looked back to the bus terminal. He scanned the crowds from left to right. Suddenly they emerged – the two men were walking hurriedly towards him. Their expressions were stern and serious. Pepito gasped. He bolted out of the store and began to sprint down the side street. He dodged several people on the street including an elderly woman selling corn out of a cart. Pepito was in a full stride when he took a sharp right turn into another unfamiliar street.

Pepito's arms were like pistons propelling him forward. His chest was pounding. The further Pepito ran, the fewer people he saw as he was heading further away from the centre of town. He finally dared to turn and look back – the two men were about 100 metres away and still rushing towards him. Pepito accelerated again and continued down the street lined with parked cars and tiny row houses.

Pepito came a bend in the road and he stepped onto the sidewalk to avoid any possible oncoming traffic. He could smell the scent of barbecue chicken as he blew past a restaurant's open door. Suddenly the road ended abruptly as it made a T-junction with a perpendicular street. Pepito came to a quick stop. Directly in front of him was the Vilconata River; he looked to his left – the road veered slightly uphill. He then looked to his right - the road continued slightly downhill parallel to the river. Each option looked the same – he didn't know which way to go. He turned around once again, the men were getting closer and he could see the expression on their faces – they looked angry and exhausted. Perhaps he could make more ground on them if he took the hilly option. Pepito turned left and pounded his way up the loose cobblestones.

The bag clanged behind him as he climbed

to the top of the hill. As soon as the road crested, Pepito stopped dead in his tracks. It was a dead end. The road ended at the base of a large concrete wall that formed the base of the bridge that spanned the river to the other side of town. Pepito was horrified. He had nowhere to go. The concrete base was tall and flat – impossible to climb and it pushed into the hillside on his left. Behind him he could hear the men scrambling up the road. Pepito took a few steps towards the river. The river was about 50 metres wide at this point and approximately five metres below the road. He could see the water rushing below – it was a sheer drop and the only thing separating Pepito from the river was a short metal guardrail. He looked to his right – the men had reached the top of the hill; they were puffing with fatigue but their eyes lit up when they saw Pepito standing there, trapped. The men, now only a few feet away, lunged towards him. Pepito was terrified, he could see the malice in their eyes – he knew he had no other option, he took a step forward, stood on top of the guardrail, clutched the bag with his right arm, and then jumped into the river below.

# CHAPTER 10

Pepito slammed into the rushing river like a torpedo. The icy waters sent shock waves through his body. He could feel the force of the river pulling him downstream, he pushed down with his legs to propel himself upwards. After several kicks, his head emerged above the surface and he let out a loud gasp. The frigid waters felt like a thousand tiny needles. Pepito scrambled for his bag – it was still there, dangling beside him. He threw the strap over his shoulder and tucked the bag between his hip and right arm. He could feel the weight of the stones pulling him down into the water. Pepito moved his arms in a circular motion to steady himself. He looked over his shoulder, the men were standing on the hillside, stunned. He angled himself sideways, pointing his body downstream. "This is not good," he thought, "I need to get out of here."

The river continued to pull him along. This was a famously fast section of the river and was popular with white water rafters and hydro-speeders. The river weaved over and around large sections of rock that protruded above the surface. Pepito braced himself by lifting his legs in the front; if he collided with a rock, his legs would hopefully absorb the impact. Pepito tried to steer himself into the centre of the river and avoid the boulders that littered the riverbank. The water was painfully cold and Pepito began to lose the feeling in his hands and feet. His teeth chattered and his body shivered.

The river veered from the adjacent road and cut through a steep gorge. The riverbank on both sides was at least twenty feet high and Pepito could only see the steep cliffs and the rock strewn, twisting river ahead. Pepito tried to calm himself, "Be patient," he thought. "There has to be a smooth spot ahead."

He continued to glide down the river narrowly avoiding the dangerous rock clusters. The numbness in his body was beginning to spread and Pepito's legs and arms began to feel increasingly heavy. He needed to find a way out, and quickly. Suddenly, up ahead, approximately 20 metres away and past the last section of rocks, the water appeared calm and flat on the surface. "Ah, thank God," said Pepito aloud, "no more rapids." He felt momentarily relieved – he could stop fighting the current and make his way to the river's edge. But his happiness was short lived. As he neared the calm waters, he suddenly saw what lay beyond: a waterfall. Pepito saw that the river dropped off some 50 feet ahead. He didn't know how far the river fell but he knew if he lost hold of the bag the Circulo was as good as gone.

Pepito frantically began paddling towards the river's edge; a few rocks to his left had created a small cove and he pushed himself in that direction. His legs and arms were like anvils – weighed down by his clothes and icy water. He forced himself to push on, combining every swim stroke he knew, hoping to reach the safety of the rocks before being swept down the waterfall. He let out a scream as he willed himself across the dangerous river. His chest pounded with pain. He could barely breathe. He swallowed short gulps of water as his head bobbed up and down below the surface.

The rocks were only a few feet away now. Pepito was exhausted. He let out another primal yell and catapulted himself towards the rocks. He reached out to grab the exposed corner of the nearest boulder; his shaking hand lifted out of the water and his fingers dug into the sharp edges. He managed to grab on. He felt relieved – he made it. He swung his other arm across his body to get a grip with both hands. Suddenly, his wet, numb fingers lost their grip on the rock and he began sliding down, away from the cove. "No!" he screamed out and lunged back upstream. Both his arms flung through the air and landed on the same exposed corner. His face and chest slammed into the face of the rock. Pain shot through him like a lightning bolt. He pulled his body up through the water and slumped onto the rock. He went limp with exhaustion.

Pepito lay there for several minutes. His breathing finally returned to normal and he could feel the fogginess in his head begin to clear. His limbs were like tree trunks, heavy and motionless. The sun was nearly setting and the cool evening air swept across his wet, exposed body. He began to shiver again and his chin started rattling off the rock face. Pepito willed himself to move. "Get up," he thought, "you need to move." He dragged his arms up to the top of the boulder and tried to lift himself up. He could barely feel his arms underneath him; it was as though his brain was sending messages to a body that wasn't responding. Pepito lifted his chest and rolled over onto the other side of the large rock. He fell between two other boulders and the bottom of the cliff wall. He was unable move, but at least now he was completely out of the river and on dry land. He knew he didn't have long before the sun would set and he would not be able to see his way out.

"Help!" he yelled out. "Please, someone help me!" He began coughing violently. "H...h... help!"

Dusk was being to settle over the gorge and the sky emitted a warm amber glow. The peaceful view contrasted sharply with Pepito's predicament. "I am not going to die here," he thought to himself, "this is not the end." He managed to lift his torso from the rocks and swiveled his legs so they could touch the ground. He pushed up with both hands and steadied himself. He was standing, a little wobbly, but standing. Pepito cupped his hands together and with all his breath yelled, "HELP!" He took two deep breaths, "HELP!" The cold air burned his lungs.

He was about to try one more time when he suddenly heard the sound of tires rolling over the terrain up above. "Hey! Help!" he shouted one more time. The car's brakes let out a short squeal as it came to a stop. Pepito could hear the gurgling of the muffler. "Help! I'm over here."

A car door opened and someone began walking towards the edge of the cliff. A single figure emerged above Pepito. The stranger looked down. Pepito could see a man – maybe in his early forties – he had a blue flannel shirt, typical of a campesino. The man edged closer and Pepito could see his face more clearly. Pepito did not know the stranger but he was struck by his expression: he seemed angry and happy all at once.

"Are you okay?" asked the stranger. "Are you hurt?"

"No, but I'm freezing and I need help to get out of here," responded Pepito.

"Hold on. I'll be right back." The man turned away and moved back to the car. He soon returned, carrying a large rope. "Tie this around your waist – I'm going to pull you out." The man threw down one end of the rope and it landed at Pepito's feet. The stranger then took the other end and looped it around the car's rear bumper. He made a knot and pulled tightly to secure it in place. The man then peered back over the cliff, "Okay, grab hold of the rope with both hands," he instructed. "Use your feet to climb up the side of the hill and I will pull you up. Got it?" Pepito nodded. He had no idea who this stranger was but he was determined that he was getting out of that gorge and back to safety.

"Here I go," said Pepito as he made his way to the wall of dirt and stone. His limbs ached and they felt like they were filled with lead but his resolve was strong. Slowly he began to inch his way up the hill. The stranger heaved and pulled, forcing the rope through his hands. The rope squeezed Pepito's midsection but he blocked out the pain and continued his way ever closer to the top. "Just put one foot in front of the other," he told himself. "One foot in front of another..."

Within moments, Pepito's head peaked above the edge of the cliff and he could see the man clearly now – he was still pulling the rope – behind him was a faded, old pick-up truck. Pepito clambered over the edge and landed on the ground only a few feet from the stranger. He felt triumphant to be out of the gorge and back on solid ground.

The man dropped his end of the rope and looked directly into Pepito's eyes. The stranger had a kind face and his eyes sparkled. He looked down at the bag and then back up to Pepito. His mood suddenly turned very serious. "You need to get out of those clothes," he said. "Take off your shirt and pants." He made his way over to the truck's cargo area and pulled out a large, tattered blanket. "Here, wrap yourself up in this, you need to warm up." The man turned from Pepito, moved towards the front of the truck and began scanning the surrounding fields. Pepito removed his heavy, wet clothes. He felt such relief as he wrapped the blanket around his body - he was still shivering and the tips of his fingers still felt numb.

"Come on. We need to go," said the man. "You need to get in the back of the truck and lie down. It's not safe for you to sit in the front and be seen. Lie down in the back – I'm going to cover you. It's important that you stay still and out of view. Don't be scared. You are safe with me. I will explain later. Do you understand?"

Pepito gave him a slight nod. "Who is this man? What does he know? Is he with them?" thought Pepito. He remained motionless, unable to process how this stranger was connected to him and the events leading to this moment.

"We have to go right now. Get in – I will explain later – I promise," the man said in a direct tone. Pepito grabbed his soggy clothes, pulled the bag over his shoulder and jumped into the cargo area. He laid down between the sidewall and two tires that lay flat on the cargo bed. The stranger pulled a blue tarp up and over Pepito and tucked the corners under the tires to keep it from blowing away. Pepito felt afraid under the darkness of the tarp. He clutched the blanket tightly. The man leaned in towards Pepito, "You are safe now," he said. "It's not a very long drive. Just be brave for a little while longer, Pepito." Pepito was stunned. The man knew his name.

"Who is he? What is going on? Where are we going?" Pepito's thoughts were interrupted by the truck's engine firing up. The truck rolled forward and began its trek across the bumpy terrain.

Time felt suspended for Pepito. He wasn't sure how long he had been in the back of the truck. Maybe ten, maybe twenty minutes. His body continuously jostled by the uneven road and the truck's aging suspension. The light was beginning to fade and darkness began to envelope Pepito in his tarp cocoon. He felt a mix of fear and anxiousness. He trusted the man and had a sense that he wasn't a part of the thugs and their plan, but many questions still swirled in his head.

Several more minutes passed and then finally, Pepito heard the brakes squeal, and the truck came to a complete stop. The man put the car in park, opened his door and moved to the side of the cargo bed. He pulled back the tarp. Pepito's eyes adjusted to the light that was shining from the house nearby. The man paused and looked at Pepito. He seemed to let out a slight smile and he had a triumphant expression on his face.

"We're here," said the man. "Come on, let's get you inside, we need to get you some dry clothes. You must be hungry, too." That was music to Pepito's ears. Although he didn't fully trust the man, more than anything right now, he needed to warm up and eat something. He scrambled out of the cargo area and landed with a thud on the dirt driveway. He looked up to see a small, modest farmhouse. A light hung above a wooden door with two matching windows on either side. The windows were covered with a thin curtain and Pepito could see a dim light coming from behind one of them. Pepito followed the man as they approached the entrance. He paused and looked around. A thick forest surrounded the stone farmhouse and the driveway wound to the rear of the property. Pepito looked back to see that the driveway continued in the other direction for about 50 metres before disappearing into a blind corner. The house was nestled into the hillside and Pepito couldn't help but wonder if he had ever seen a more remote property. He took a deep breath and continued towards the door. The man had been standing there waiting for him with one hand on the door knob.

"Ready?" asked the man, a smile spreading across his face. Pepito wasn't sure what he meant. "Ready for what?" he thought. Pepito ascended the two stone steps leading towards the doorway and stepped inside. All his fears and concerns were laid to rest as soon as he entered the tiny entrance. For the second time in as many days, there waiting with open arms, was his mother.

# CHAPTER 11

"**S**it down in here... by the fire," said Rosita. "I have some soup and bread." She led Pepito into the kitchen and guided him to a chair by the wood burning stove. "I'll get you something to wear." Pepito fell into the small, wooden chair. He wasn't sure if it was the heat coming from the stove, or seeing his mother, but he once again felt the energy return to his weary body.

Rosita and the man stepped into the kitchen and stood together in front of Pepito. Rosita carried a folded shirt and pants. They both paused and stared at Pepito. Rosita looked at the man, then at Pepito, and then back to the man again. Pepito could see her eyes beginning to water and then tears began to streak down her face. The man leaned across and held Rosita in his arms; he too had water pooling in his eyes. They embraced for a moment before composing themselves and turning back towards Pepito.

"We will talk in just a moment," said Rosita. "Put these on and get something in your stomach first." Rosita handed Pepito the clothes and prepared him a bowl of soup. The scent of chicken and beans wafted through the air; Pepito was ravaged with hunger. He threw on the jeans and flannel shirt – they were both a little big, but Pepito didn't mind – he was just glad to wear something warm and dry again. He sat back down and devoured his meal in an instant. Soup and bread never tasted so good. Pepito finished his glass of milk and then sat back in the chair, relieved to be feeling normal again. His focus redirected back to his mother and the stranger – they were now sitting around him at the small kitchen table.

"Feel better?" asked Rosita as she cleared the bowl from the table. "Things are always easier after soup." Rosita smiled at Pepito and shuffled her chair close to his. "I want you to take your time and tell me everything that happened since this morning, okay sweetie? Don't leave out any details, okay? It's important we know exactly where you went and who you saw..."

Rosita refilled his glass of milk and Pepito began to retell the events that happened between the moment he woke up and the time he heard the stranger's car on the clifftop above the river. As he described the events, Rosita and the strange man exchanged knowing looks and nodded repeatedly at each other. Rosita appeared worried and wrung her hands as Pepito described the final dangerous moments in the river. She felt guilty knowing he was in such danger.

When Pepito finished, he looked to the strange man and then back at his mother. "I don't mean to be rude but, who is this man? How do you know him and how did he know I was there at the river?" Rosita closed her eyes for a moment to consider her words. She knew she had to choose her words carefully. She opened her eyes again and placed her hands on top of his.

"Pepito," she began, "this might be difficult for you to hear and it might be very upsetting but the time has come to tell you about us, all of us, and all the things we have been keeping from you."

"Keeping from me?" Pepito questioned.

"Pepito...Pepito, this is Jose Inti Capac...senior. This... this is your father..." The words seemed suspended in the air – Pepito heard them, but they didn't register.

"But... how... I thought..." he stammered.

"We told you, and everyone else, a story to protect you – to protect all three of us. It was something we had to do. But things are different now..." Rosita turned to Jose, "Do you want to..." Jose nodded and dragged his chair closer to Pepito.

"Pepito, first you need to know that, yes, I am your dad – I have always been your dad and the reason I... well... the reason I... let me start at the beginning," said Jose. He cleared his throat and sighed heavily. "Okay. When I was a young man I entered the military – my goal was to serve and honour our great country. I spent several years in various posts throughout the country and before I knew it, I had risen to the position of Senior Captain. I worked hard and showed that I could be relied upon in different situations. Soon after, my Colonel assigned me to do some intelligence work, and specifically, counter-terrorism, and I was doing more and more undercover, behind the scenes kind of duty. When I was stationed in Lima, I met your mother, your beautiful mother, and after a while, we decided to get married. I thought I would be in Lima for some time so we planned to stay there and raise a family. Well we did get married and it was a great day – we were so happy and excited about our future. But then soon after that, everything changed.

I was at work one day when the General of the Federal Army called me to say that he wanted to see me. He said two secret service agents would pick me up and take me to meet him and some others in a private location. I knew it must've been important but I had no idea what was ahead of me when I arrived at the meeting. They took me to a government building and then down an elevator five floors underground. They led me past several security check points before finally leading me to a thick metal door. To my surprise, behind the door was a long table and at the far end sat the President of Peru. Of course, I was in awe of seeing him, and at that point I realized that my career was about to take a drastic turn.

He sat me down and told me how impressed he was with my work and that I had shown great honour and integrity in my duties. He then asked me if I knew what a Shadow Runner was. You see, Pepito, when the mighty Incas ruled this land, the kings and high priests would enlist a few men – courageous and clever men – to protect and pass along their most prized possessions and documents. The rulers would send the Shadow Runners between villages and towns. Their job was to keep the items not only safe, but also a secret from all others. They were the first spies our country has known."

Jose shifted in his seat and took a sip of water from a glass that sat on the table. He then continued, "When the Spanish invaded our land, the Shadow Runners were responsible for keeping our valuables from the conquistadors, and they were entrusted to keep the secrets of Machu Picchu, including its location, and most importantly, the secrets of the Casa Del Oro. The four most daring Runners were entrusted with the Clave Circulo – each one was given a stone and they were instructed to protect it with their lives. Luckily, the conquistadors never found the Clave and the location of the Casa Del Oro, but they, and generations of thieves, have never stopped trying."

"Is that what you are? Are you a Shadow Runner?" asked Pepito.

"Yes. I am the present-day version... so... that morning, in the meeting with the President, he offered me the position and explained the responsibilities associated with the job. Typically, Shadow Runners live secretly and unknown to the public. While some are married, they never, or in some cases rarely, have children. And so, that was the case with us. I accepted the position and then within just a few weeks we discovered that your mother was pregnant with you. We decided that I should stay in the position – it is such an honour to be chosen to protect your country – I just couldn't say no... soon after you were born, we were assigned to live in Arequipa... and... during the early years, things were fairly normal, we lived together and we were a normal, happy family. But then, when you were three years old, our greatest fear became a reality."

"What? What happened?" asked Pepito. Jose took a deep breath and looked across at Rosita. Her eyes were once again beginning to water. She nodded reassuringly, encouraging Jose to continue.

"A group of criminals from outside the country began to follow me and your mother. We noticed them several times in various locations as we went about our daily routines. And then one day... one day they attempted to kidnap you."

"Why would they do that?" asked Pepito.

"For the same reason the Sempre gang tried to kidnap you now – they want to use my family to get the Clave Circulo." Suddenly a cloud of uncertainty cleared from Pepito's mind. The pieces of the puzzle were finally falling into place.

"What happened with the first gang?" he asked.

Jose stopped and looked at the ground. He cleared his throat again and sat up in the chair. "We were able to stop that first group before they could get to you, and fortunately, we were able to apprehend them, and to this day, they are still locked away in a federal prison... but it was at that time that we realized we needed to make some changes to protect you. We were reassigned to live in Cuzco and I began to live a secret life, away from you and your mom, and we told people that I went to prison to avoid revealing my cover. But I have always been a part of your life, and I have seen you grow up – except I did it from a distance - hiding in the shadows. I was there for your first day of kindergarten, I was there when you scored your first soccer goal with the school team, and I was there recently when you celebrated your Confirmation. I have always been there for you... you just didn't know it..." Rosita leaned across the table and took Jose's hand in hers.

"Your father loves you very much," she said. "His duties kept us apart physically but he has always been in our hearts. Do you understand that, Pepito? Do you understand why we did the things we had to do?" Pepito looked at his mother. He had known her so well for his entire life and now there were so many more layers to her that were completely unknown.

"Yes, yes I do," began Pepito. "I'm actually really impressed and amazed. Before now, I thought my dad was a criminal, and now I find out that he is one of the most important people in our country. That is pretty cool." Both Jose and Rosita let out a small laugh.

"Yes, it is pretty cool," said Rosita as she took Pepito's hand.

"So, who are the thugs that came after me this time?" asked Pepito.

Jose's expression turned serious again. "Those men that took you... they are very dangerous and they obviously are after the Clave."

"Do you know anything about them?" asked Pepito.

"Yes... they are members of the Sempre gang. You saw three men last night, right?" Pepito nodded. "Well, the heavier man, the driver of the car, his name is Alberto, but they call him 'El Toro' - the Bull. The man that grabbed you in the plaza his name is Ramon, but he goes by the nickname 'Gitano' - the Gypsy. The man who spoke to you – the leader – his name is Ruiz. He is commonly known as 'El Cicatrizado' - the scarred one, but most of time he goes by 'El Cica' or just 'Cica'. Cica is the mastermind behind the gang and their criminal activity. He is dangerous, very dangerous, not only because he is willing to break any law to achieve his goal, but he is also an intelligent and clever thinker. He is well informed and in possession of a lot of important information."

"What do you mean? Is he a genius criminal or something?" asked Pepito.

"Not exactly," replied Jose. "He is actually someone I have known for a very long time... when he was around your age, he was just a street kid. He had run away from an abusive home and he was living on the streets – sometimes begging and sometimes stealing to feed himself and get by. An old friend of mine, Senhor Garcia, had seen the boy on the street several times and decided to help him. He began buying him meals and new clothes to stay warm in winter, and after some time, Senhor Garcia became attached to the young Cica and eventually brought him home to live with him and his wife. They didn't have any kids and they raised the boy as if he was their own and they, too, tried to be a normal, regular family. But things don't always work out the way you planned... Although he had a roof over his head and all the things needed to live a normal life, Cica was never happy. He frequently fought with Senhora Garcia and he was constantly getting in trouble at school for fighting or stealing from the other children."

"Why was he so angry?" asked Pepito.

"I'm not sure. Perhaps he never felt like he belonged in the Garcia family or maybe it was the abuse he suffered as a young child, but whatever it was, he always had a bitterness about him. Senhor Garcia did his best and he spent several years trying to keep him out of trouble. When he was about 18 or so, Cica began his involvement with the local gangs in El Campo and Senhor Garcia was worried that he would lose Cica to the gang world. There was a period of about three years when Senhor Garcia didn't see or speak to Cica. But then things changed. After a while, Cica contacted Senhor Garcia and they began to talk once again. It took time, but their relationship developed and they actually became close. Senhor Garcia started trusting Cica, who now seemed like a different person – more mature and content with life and himself. I remember Senhor Garcia was so happy when he believed their past troubles were behind them..."

Jose paused. He looked down at the floor and rubbed his eyes. He took a short breath and continued.

"But of course they weren't. Cica won back Senhor Garcia's trust and pretended to be a loving son because - because he knew Senhor Garcia was a Shadow Runner." Pepito's mouth widened.

"What? He was one of the four Shadow Runners?"

"Yes," replied Jose. "Cica spent his time collecting information about the Clave and planning his attack. He took Senhor Garcia's trust and used it to locate the other pieces and figure out a way to collect them. We didn't see it coming – it all happened so fast. This occurred in just a matter of days - these past few days. The thugs used kidnapping and blackmail to acquire the pieces and this is all going on because they want to have the pieces for the equinox that will occur tomorrow at noon. They are desperate to have the Clave at the altar in Machu Picchu to locate the Casa Del Oro."

Jose paused and looked down at the floor. The stress and pressure of the last few days had taken a toll on him. His struggle to do his job and do what is best for his family clearly weighed heavily on his shoulders. He took a moment to regain his composure.

"But don't you worry. We will handle this. We will handle everything," he said reassuringly.

"And what about those two guys on the bus – the ones that chased me into the river?" questioned Pepito.

"They are Cruz and Castillo; two other members of Cica's gang. They work in the Sacred Valley mostly, running most of the gang's illegal activity in that area. They are known for extorting and intimidating the local farmers."

"Okay. That's enough for tonight," stated Rosita. "You must be exhausted, sweetie. Come, you need to get some rest. Tomorrow is another day and we can discuss things then." She stood up from the table and took Pepito by the arm, "Come, your bed is in here, I'll show you."

Pepito stood up; his legs wobbled beneath him. His head was spinning from all the information. Although he had more questions about his father and his past, he knew he was too tired to think clearly. The one thought that was abundantly clear: he couldn't wait to lie down on that bed.

# CHAPTER 12

March 20th, 8:04am

Pepito ambled into the kitchen, still rubbing the sleep out of his eyes. He slept soundly all night and he was feeling much more energized. Rosita and Jose were sitting at the table sorting through some cell phones and other electronic devices.

"Good morning, Pepito," said Jose looking up from the table.

"Have some breakfast," Rosita said as she pointed to a plate filled with eggs, potatoes and rice. "How are you feeling? Did you sleep well?"

"Yeah, I did. I don't even remember falling asleep," answered Pepito.

"Yesterday was a very long day for you," said Rosita as she poured a glass. "Here, have some juice, too."

"Thanks," said Pepito taking his seat in the chair. "What are all these things?"

"Communication devices," answered Jose. "There are a few things I need to show..."

"Let him eat first. The boy just woke up," said Rosita smiling comfortingly at Pepito.

Pepito smiled back and nodded. He then proceeded to devour his breakfast. His hunger for food was surpassed by his hunger to learn more about the craft of being a Shadow Runner.

"Okay, I'm done," Pepito muffled through a mouthful of eggs. He took one last sip of juice. "I'm ready."

Jose let out a slight grin. He was amused and secretly proud of Pepito's enthusiasm. He held up a cell phone with an unusually thick plastic cover. "This is a military grade cell phone. You can drop it from a hundred feet and it will still work." He handed it to Pepito. "This is yours to use to get in touch with us. There are three preset phone numbers. Number one is to contact me, number two is your mother, and number three is our central safe house in Cusco."

Pepito's eyes widened as he took the phone into his hands.

"Now this is very important," continued Jose. "Only call the third number if you cannot get in touch with your mother or me. And more importantly, only use the phone in case of emergency. And most importantly, do not let anyone else use the phone – ever. It must not fall into the wrong hands. Understand?" Pepito nodded reassuringly.

"The next thing I need to show you is over here." Jose stood up and walked into the other bedroom at the rear of the house. He led Pepito to the far side of the bed that sat in the centre of the small room. The old wooden floors creaked as they walked. Jose knelt down by the bed and pulled back the rectangular rug that ran the length of the bed. Pepito came around to get a better view. Jose then took out his pocket knife, unfolded the blade and delicately placed it between two planks on the floor. Jose tilted the blade and gently lifted the floor board away from the others. He placed the board on the floor and asked Pepito to come closer. Pepito leaned in. Over his father's shoulder he could see a digital keypad in the space left by the removed board. He was amazed to see such a modern device in such a rustic location.

"Now the code should be easy for you to remember – it's the month and day of your birthday," said Jose moving aside to make room for Pepito. "Give it a try."

Pepito slid up to the mysterious keypad in the floor. He leaned in and waved his fingers over the buttons. "October 21. So, that's 1021," he thought. Pepito pushed his fingers into the buttons. For a moment, nothing happened. Pepito looked at Jose.

"Just give it a second," said Jose.

Then suddenly the floor boards beneath the bed began to move. A section a few feet long began to drop and slide underneath the rest of the floor. Pepito gasped. He couldn't believe what he saw. The boards stopped moving to reveal a square opening directly underneath the bed. Pepito tried to lean in to see inside the cavity but it was too dark to make anything out.

"There is a small crawl space inside," Jose stated. "Just enough room for a couple of people. There is a shelf on the nearest wall. The Clave is there and that's where we will keep it until we need to move it." Pepito had completely forgotten about the Clave since last night. "This is where you hide in case something happens, okay? We should be fine but I want to show you in the event of an emergency. There is another keypad above the shelf inside that will allow you to open and close the door."

"Wow. This is amazing. I can't believe what I'm seeing," said Pepito, bewildered.

"But remember - everything remains a secret to everyone but me and your mother."

Pepito nodded. "Just amazing..." he muttered.

Jose sealed the door, replaced the floor board, pulled the rug back to its original position and led Pepito back to the kitchen. Rosita was putting away the last of the dishes from breakfast. Pepito was surprised to see everything had been tidied so quickly. Rosita turned and moved towards Pepito.

"Sweetie... your father and I... we have to go

now."

"Where are you going?" asked Pepito.

"We need to get back to Cusco. We need to keep an eye on Cica and monitor his activity," replied Jose. "We don't want to leave you but we don't have much time and we can't afford to let him get away from us."

"But what if he comes here? What if he comes after me?" pleaded Pepito.

"We have reports that he is currently at the gang hangout in El Campo. The sooner we get into town, the sooner we can protect you from him," said Jose, placing his hand on Pepito's shoulder. "I am so proud of you and you have shown tremendous bravery. Trust me, we have to do this, there is no other choice."

Pepito looked at his mother. She wore a concerned look on her face. She wanted to stay and protect her son but she felt safe knowing Cica was miles away and unaware of their whereabouts. Going after Cica and the gang was the best way to protect not only Pepito, but the Clave too.

Pepito could see that his parents were firm in their decision and he knew there were greater concerns than his need to be with them right now.

"Alright," he said, "do what you have to. I'll be okay."

"This will be over soon, sweetie," Rosita said, kissing him on the forehead.

"Keep the phone with you," reminded Jose. "We will be back soon and hopefully this entire situation will be behind us. The solstice is at noon today. We need to keep the gang away from here and the Clave until then. After that, they won't be a threat to you or anyone else." Jose patted Pepito on the shoulder and gave Pepito a long reassuringly look before slowly making his way towards the door.

Pepito watched as his parents closed the door behind them and headed towards the parked truck. He watched through the small window as the truck rolled down the driveway and disappeared into the bend in the road. Pepito turned back into the kitchen. He looked down at the large cell phone that sat on the table. He then looked down at the clothes he was wearing. He hadn't realized that he still wore the oversized shirt and pants his mother gave him the night before. Pepito moved into the bedroom where his clothes had been hung to dry in the narrow closet. He pulled down his sweater and jeans. He was disappointed to see that they were still damp in places.

Pepito decided to dry the clothes in the sun and went outside to find a suitable spot. There was no clothesline in sight, so Pepito scanned the property looking for another option. Finally, he spotted a large rock near the edge of the driveway that was baking in sunlight. He spread out his clothes on the rock, and feeling content with himself, ventured back inside.

He sat down at the kitchen table and picked up the cell phone. Even though the phone had a metallic body and sturdy plastic case, it was surprisingly light for its size. He examined the edges, searching for the power button. Once he found it, he pressed firmly and the phone came to life. Pepito marveled at the device. Young boys in Cusco, particularly the ones Pepito knew, rarely had cell phones and he felt buoyed by the thought that he now possessed such a special item.

He examined the screen. The cellular reception was not very strong, only two bars were lit and there were only two icons on the home screen: "contacts" and "GPS". Pepito tapped the contacts icon and there, like his father said, were three contacts listed in numerical order. He closed the window and tapped the GPS icon. The window opened and revealed a map with a single street and an arrow indicating "your location" where the road seemed to begin. Pepito zoomed out to get a better look at the street's surroundings. The map, now more detailed and comprehensive, showed the road led to a dead end not far from the house. There was a short gap before another street ran perpendicular to the road. "Maybe it's a bridge or unfinished track that's between the two roads," thought Pepito. He looked at the area surrounding the house. The map showed that there was nothing in the vicinity and the house was quite isolated from the rest of the neighbouring terrain.

Pepito slid the screen to the right to try and locate the river and see the path they might have taken in the truck last night. He was impressed by how far the river was from the property. There were very few roads labeled on the map so their journey must have been through unmarked paths and open fields.

Pepito slid the screen to the left to determine what lay in the other direction. He didn't slide for too long before he was taken aback by what he saw. Off to the west, beyond what looked like barren land, was the site of Machu Picchu. Pepito had no idea he was so close. He attempted to zoom in and out to determine the distance between the house and the infamous ruins. It didn't appear to be too far away but there weren't any visible roads linking the two locations. Pepito zoomed closer. Finally, he made out a swerving path that led from the rear part of Machu Picchu towards the direction of the house. He zoomed in again. It looked like a trail that followed a circular route that continued past the house and eventually made its way to the river. Pepito scanned through the settings before locating the "terrain" feature. He clicked on it and discovered that the trail wove across the mountains and seemed to undulate up and over several valleys. "This must be the Inca Trail," he thought. "The trail used by the original Shadow Runners to relay messages between Machu Picchu and the villages." He typed "Machu Picchu" into the "destination" bar and the map revealed a distance of 5.4 kilometres from the ruins to the house. "Wow.

Not that far," he thought.

Pepito put down the phone and sat back in his chair. He shook his head, bewildered by all the events that had happened the past few days. His life to this point had been predictable and unexciting, and now, within a 36-hour period, he had been kidnapped, stolen the single greatest item in Peruvian history, been chased by thugs into a rushing river, and had been saved by his father – who just happens to be an infamous Shadow Runner and not a convicted criminal. So much to process. Pepito felt a little overwhelmed by the process of trying to fill in the missing gaps of the past fourteen years, so instead, he told himself to take things slowly and let the answers come in time.

He stood up and made his way outside to see if his clothes were ready. He ventured out the door and down the driveway towards the large rock. He picked up his jeans and sweater. "Almost, but not quite dry," he thought. He was about to place the clothes back on the rock when suddenly he heard the sound of a car rolling along the crushed gravel off behind the distant trees. The car's engine whined as it made its way along the uneven driveway.

Pepito froze. He knew this wasn't Jose's truck. Pepito grabbed his clothes and bolted up the driveway and back towards the house.

# CHAPTER 13

**M**arta spent most of Saturday trying to keep herself busy and her thoughts occupied. Her mother was surprised to see her so willing to do housework. Martha washed the floors, cleaned the bathrooms and even helped prepare dinner. She did almost anything to get her mind off those thugs and whatever danger was threatening Pepito.

She wanted so badly to tell her mother about the kidnapping and the mysterious car that sped past her but she remembered Rosita instructions. She was not to tell anyone – not even the police. Rosita had been like a second mother and she trusted her wholeheartedly. No matter how strange and unusual Rosita's words were on Friday night, she knew it was best for everyone to abide by her requests.

It was now Sunday morning and Marta sat at the kitchen table staring listlessly at the eggs on her plate. She had spent a restless night tossing and turning with worry and her eyes felt heavy, like they were filled with sand. She couldn't help but feel useless and trapped.

"Aren't you hungry?" asked her mother from the sink. "You've barely touched your breakfast."

"No... not really," said Marta despondently.

"Is everything okay?"

"Yeah, I'm just not in the mood to eat right now," responded Marta.

"Well then put the food in a container. You can always eat it later when you get hungry."

"Sure," Marta replied with a bit of feigned enthusiasm. She did not want her mother to suspect that something was bothering her. Her mom had a knack of knowing when she was upset and keeping things private. "I didn't have a great sleep last night, so I'm just a little tired..." Marta said as she stood up from her chair with her plate in hand.

"Maybe you can have a nap later in the afternoon," said her mother.

"Yeah... maybe," said Marta as she took out a plastic container from the bottom cupboard.

Marta's mother continued to clean the dishes. "I'm going to the grocery store soon to get a few things," she said. "Your dad is coming home around lunch time – the repair job should only take him a couple of hours... do you want anything in particular from the store?"

"More mangoes? The ones you bought last week were really good," said Marta positively.

"I'll look for some more," said her mother as she dried her hands with a hand towel. "I'll also try and stich your jacket later – I noticed the thread is coming loose around the collar."

"Thanks. That would be good," said Marta putting the container in the fridge.

Within a few minutes, Marta's mom was out the door on her way to the store. Marta sat back down on the kitchen chair and looked blankly at the wall in front of her. Her gaze drew slowly to the calendar that hung on the wall above the dining table. She looked at the picture that hung above the row of dates for the month of March. It was a photo of a sunset in the Plaza de Armas s-quare, but it looked more like a painting with soft, warm waves of orange and blue floating in the night sky. Marta was suddenly reminded of the horror she experienced in that very square just two days ago. Her stomach clenched like a tight fist and anger swelled in her chest. Her mind raced once again with thoughts of the thugs and what they wanted with her best friend. More un-certainty added to her already high levels of fear and frustration. She glanced away from the pic-ture and down the calendar. She looked aimlessly at the rows of numbers and days of the week. She paused when she locked on today's date. It was March 20 – the spring equinox. Today was no or-dinary day. Her heart beat rapidly and her stom-ach churned. "Is this a clue?" she thought. "Does this mean something?"

Pepito was constantly poking fun at Marta for being superstitious. He enjoyed mocking the fact that she never stepped on the lines surrounding the soccer field, and she always did the sign of the cross three times when they passed a church. But she always felt like she had an intuitive sense about things and the world around her. He saw it as fun and games, but Marta knew she had a cosmic connection that others couldn't understand.

She looked closer at the calendar. There is no way that this is just a coincidence that there would be a picture of the Plaza de Armas and that she would notice that today is the equinox. Something in the universe must be trying to send her a message. "But what is the message?" she thought. "What does this mean?"

There was only one person that could help her. Feeling inspired, Marta stood and strode over to the small desk in the corner of the kitchen. She pulled out a pen and paper and began to write, "I went to Senhor Gonzalez' house. Be back later. Kisses. M."

Marta then grabbed her coat and went to the front window. She looked up and down the street. Everything was quiet and the street was clear of any cars. Marta decided it best not to use the front door, just in case. She went through the back door and across her small backyard. She hopped the low- lying metal fence and walked quickly to the side of her rear neighbour's house. She walked between the houses and emerged on the other side. She reached the sidewalk on Calle Aventura and turned right to make her way to the nearby cross street. Once she arrived at the intersection, she crossed the street and stood under the pole marking the #12 bus stop. She waited anxiously for the bus that would take her to San Blas.

# CHAPTER 14

Pepito raced to the house, adrenalin shot him towards the front door like a cannon. He quickly opened it, stepped inside and closed it behind him as stealthy as he could. He slowly raised his head above the base of the small window in the centre of the door. He didn't see anything but he could hear the car's engine as it came closer to the property.

Then suddenly, a blue, older model sedan with rusty patches emerged from the trees and made its way down the long driveway. The car bounced over the rough surface and the engine strained itself to keep up with the driver's urgent pace. The car came closer and closer, but Pepito couldn't get a good look at the occupants – it looked like a driver and one passenger but the glare off the windshield kept their faces obscured. Pepito wondered if perhaps it was someone sent by his parents to help him. Maybe another undercover spy or government worker who was sent to protect him.

The car reached the house and stopped. Pepito still could not make out their identities. The car doors opened and two men stepped out. Pepito's head snapped back in horror. It was Cruz and Castillo -the two men that chased him into the river!

Pepito stepped back from the door. Fear once again stiffened his limbs. He took a series of short, quick breaths. "What should I do...?" he thought panic stricken. "What should I do...? The trap door!" He quickly darted into the bedroom at the rear of the house, lunged into the room and made a hard turn around the far side of the bed where the keypad lay. He dropped his clothes on the floor, violently pulled back the rug, and zeroed in on the wooden plank that concealed the pad. He spotted the board and dug his fingers into the gap to lift it upward, but the board did not move. He could hear the men's voices outside. They were just outside the front door. Pepito's heart thumped in his chest. He needed something to pry open the board, but he couldn't take a chance going into the kitchen for a knife. He looked around the room – nothing around him was small or thin enough to fit in the opening. Pepito could no longer hear the men speaking, he wasn't sure what they were up to. He put his two hands along the board's edge and pushed down on all ten fingers. He slid his fingernails into the gap and tilted his hands to lift up the board.

Suddenly the knob on the front door turned and Pepito could hear it creak as it opened. In his state of panic, Pepito had forgotten to lock the door.

Pepito's hands were shaking violently but he steadied himself long enough to get a grip on the board with his fingernails and slowly lifted the board out of the floor. He could hear the men shuffling into the front of the house. With his left hand gripping the board, he used his right hand to punch in the four-digit code. The two seconds that passed felt like an eternity. Finally, the trap door began to move and slide its way across the floor. Pepito prayed that the men couldn't hear the quiet hiss of the hydraulic pistons. He could hear them whispering to each other – they must be in the kitchen by now. Pepito placed the board back into its place and climbed as quickly and quietly as possible into the crawl space beneath the bed. His feet touched down about three feet below the wood floor. He scrambled forward to grab his clothes and the rug that lay crumpled at the foot of the bed. The men were moving again and Pepito could hear footsteps in the front bedroom. He threw his clothes in the crawl space and extended the rug back to its original position. The men were now back in the kitchen and moving towards the rear bedroom. They were coming towards him.

Pepito slid into the small opening and lowered his head below the floorboards. He could barely see his hands in front of his face. He felt blind and helpless. His eyes darted up and down the opening. Finally, he spotted a dimly lit fluorescent keypad to his far left. He locked in on the keypad and once again pushed the four buttons as quickly as he could. The trap door did not move. Pepito could hear the footsteps – they were in the bedroom doorway. He lifted his head above the floor. He could see a pair of heavy black boots enter the room and pass along the far edge of the bed. He ducked underneath and tried the buttons one more time. One. Zero. Two. One. The man moved to the end of the bed. Pepito did not dare move or even breath, he sat completely still. Finally, the familiar hiss sounded and the trap door began to slide its way back again.

"Did you hear that?" asked the man at the bottom of the bed.

"Hear what?" asked the other thug who was still in the kitchen.

The man in the room didn't respond, instead he moved along the side of the bed where the rug lay. Pepito did not flinch. The door continued to glide across the floor – inching its way along. The man stopped halfway down the bed and paused. He looked around the room – trying to locate the source of the hum. He sensed it was coming from underneath the bed. He knelt down with one knee and braced himself on the edge of the mattress. Pepito gasped as he saw the knee drop just a few feet away from his face. The trap door was just inches from closing. "So close now," thought Pepito. The man lowered his portly body and craned his neck below the bottom of the bed. Just as the space underneath the mattress came into his view, the trap door locked back in place.

Pepito was as still as a statue – his entire body was completely motionless. The man also did not move. The two of them sat there for several moments, hidden from each other. Pepito was enveloped in fear and darkness.

"Did I hear what?" asked the man impatiently from the kitchen.

The man in the bedroom lifted himself up from the wooden floor. "Nothing. I thought I heard something... maybe it was the generator kicking on... Looks like the place is clean, no one here."

"What should we do about this phone?" asked the thug.

The portly man walked back into the kitchen to take a closer look at the cell phone left on the table. Pepito felt slightly relieved but upset with himself for forgetting the phone.

"Let's call Cica and see what he says," said the portly man. "I'm pretty sure he's going to want to hear about this." Castillo took out his phone and called his gang leader. Pepito tried to sit as motionless as possible in the dark hole but he could feel his hands shaking with fear.

"Cica it's me, Castillo. Listen, we searched the area like you told us and we found a house... well we kind of found it by accident. We stopped by the side of the road because Cruz had to take a leak and that's when we saw a house through the trees. It was in the middle of nowhere and we couldn't even find the road that connected to the house. We finally came across a gate that was covered with bushes and stuff. We opened the gate and we found an old road that took us to this house."

Castillo paused while Cica spoke. After a brief moment, he continued. "No one is here and the place is clean but we did find a phone just sitting here on the kitchen table – it's not a regular cell phone, it's kind of big and fancy looking... Okay, sounds good... Sure... Okay, we will see you there." Castillo hung up the phone and turned to Cruz. "Cica wants us to meet him at Aguas Calientes. He's on his way right now."

"Alright, let's go," replied Cruz.

Castillo grabbed the cell phone from the table and the two men moved towards the door. Pepito listened carefully as they exited the house and made their way towards their car. The thugs jumped in the clunky vehicle, did a u turn, and then proceeded down the driveway away from the house. The car once again wheezed its way over the uneven driveway.

Pepito let out a slow, deep breath. He looked around the dark space but the soft light emitting from the glow in the keypad provided very little light for him to see. He felt the space around him. The walls and floor were cool to the touch and surprisingly smooth, like they had been polished. He continued to feel the wall in front of him until he came across a narrow opening in the wall. He fumbled about until he felt the familiar fabric of his shoulder bag. He pulled it out and felt the weight of the stones inside as the bag slipped to the bottom of the crawl space. He felt safe now and assumed the thugs were far enough away from the house. Pepito entered the four-digit code into the keypad and waited for the trap door to slide open. He grabbed the bag and his clothes off the floor, climbed out of the space and slid under the bed to the far side of the bedroom. He closed the trap door and quickly changed back into his own clothes.

He paused for a minute and stood calmly in the centre of the bedroom. He took several deep breaths and tried to carefully determine what he should do next. He peered out the window – the thugs' car appeared to be long gone and there was no sign of anyone or anything. "What should I do? What can I do?" he thought. Pepito glanced down at the canvas bag laying on the floor. He needed to protect the Clave Circulo and not let it get into the wrong hands. He also needed to get in touch with his parents and inform them about the thugs. Cruz and Castillo knew the location of the house and the phone might lead them to his parents. Cica might do something to his parents – he's probably desperate enough to turn violent. Pepito was distraught and uncertain what to do.

He looked at the clock on the bedside table. It read 10:00 am. Only two hours remained until the noonday sun would cast its light on the infamous altar that showed the way towards the Casa Del Oro. There was only two hours between finding the Casa or letting it remain hidden for another year... Pepito had to get the Clave out of the house and as far away from the thugs as possible... "What should I do?" He thought again. Suddenly, he made up his mind. He couldn't resist the temptation, he had to at least try...

Pepito picked up the bag off the table and strode towards the front door. He felt more and more confident as he exited the house and turned towards the hillside at the rear of the property. Pepito followed a path between some trees and climbed to the summit of the hill. He reached the top and looked around. The trees obscured most of the view in his vicinity. He scanned the ground around him until he finally spotted what he was looking for. About 20 feet to the north was a patch of exposed dirt that appeared to be the trail. With a very determined first step, he pushed back the bushes and started on the trail that would lead him, hopefully, to Machu Picchu.

# CHAPTER 15

Rosita and Jose hopped into the pick-up truck and spent the first few minutes riding in silence. They were both filled with excitement that the family was together again and Jose was finally able to see his son face to face – an experience that eluded him for a decade. They were equally anxious to return to Pepito and begin their new life as a united family, but right now, there were more pressing issues to contend with. Cica and his men posed a threat not only to their family, but to the entire nation. They had to be found and they had to be stopped.

Rosita took out her cell phone and tapped the phone number listed simply as 'number five' under her favourites. She then hit 'speaker' and waited impatiently as the phone rang twice, then three times, then four... finally a familiar voice answered.

"This is Javier."

"Any news?" asked Rosita urgently.

"No. Status Quo. Still no activity," responded Javier. "The gang is still holed up inside. Diego is still out front and we haven't seen them come or go since last night."

"What about the sentinels? Have you talked with them?" pressed Rosita.

"Yeah. They've been checking in every ten minutes or so. Still no sign of them on the roads either."

Javier and Diego were the third and fourth Shadow Runners responsible for protecting the Clave Circulo. Once Rosita and Jose were aware of the kidnapping, Javier and Diego set up a lookout behind the thugs' hideout in the Castro. Javier was keeping a close eye on the rear entrance by hiding in a nearby garage and Diego was monitoring the front entrance from a laundromat across the street. The sentinels were a group of three military guards that were instructed to keep a lookout for Cica and his gang along the three roads that led out of Cusco towards Machu Picchu.

Rosita continued her inquiry, "So no one has come in or gone out at all from the building?"

"No. No one," replied Javier. "Well, there was a kid delivering a package about a half hour ago. But he was lost, kept knocking on different doors, probably had the wrong address."

Rosita suddenly grew concerned. "What kind of package? What exactly did you see?"

"It was out front so I only know what Diego told me...a kid... a delivery kid, with DHL Express

I think, drove up in a delivery truck and parked down the street. He had a small cardboard box with him. He kept checking the box and the house addresses along the street. He knocked on a few doors, including the gang hideout, and then he got back in the truck and drove off with the package still in hand."

Jose and Rosita thought pensively for a moment. Finally, Jose asked, "Javier, what was he wearing?"

"The uniform – yellow and red jacket with dark pants," answered Javier.

"Did he have a hat on?" asked Jose.

"Yeah a ball cap. A company one – also red and yellow."

Jose grit his teeth and shook his head. "Did the delivery guy go inside the hideout?"

"Yeah, but he just stepped inside for a second and then left," Javier stated.

Jose gripped the wheel tightly, "Dammit... dammit..." He muttered under his breath. "Javi – it's a decoy. The guy traded places with Cica when he went into the hideout...I knew they were up to something... did you get a look at him – or did Diego get a look at him after he left the hideout?"

"Not sure, I can call him," answered Javier flatly, suddenly feeling despondent for letting Jose and Rosita down.

"That's okay – doesn't matter. Look, change of plans. Tell the Sentinels to be on the lookout for the DHL truck... he had a half hour head start so he's probably past them on his way to Machu Picchu now. We are going to Ollantaytambo – going to get there before him and cut him off at the pass. Stay where you are and keep me informed of anything – you hear me? Anything."

"Yes, of course," replied Javier. "Jose, I am so sorry for letting this happen. The last thing I want to do is let you down."

"Don't worry. We still have time. I really didn't expect them to make this easy anyway. Don't blame yourself or Diego. Just stay focused and ready for anything. I, we, really need you."

Rosita hung up the phone as Jose pressed down on the accelerator.

# CHAPTER 16

Pepito looked up the trail as it meandered away from the property.

What he didn't see was the rusted car that was parked in a dense section of forest approximately 300 metres from the farmhouse. The thugs had waited in hiding and watched Pepito as he left the house and disappeared into the forest.

Pepito took a deep breath and took his first steps along the dirt path. He knew he would have to move quickly; the Inca Trail was notoriously challenging and time consuming. He had less than two hours to make the journey. From what he remembered, the trail was fairly flat near the river but became steeper as it approached Machu Picchu. He was far enough from the river to know that he was in for a daunting 5.4 kilometres.

He walked briskly as the trail began to slowly ascend in front of him. He looked up at a sky clear of clouds as the warm sun shone brightly above. The trail was calm and quiet;

a peaceful path surrounded by tall trees and even taller mountains. The Inca Trail passed through and among some of the most striking parts of the Peruvian Andes. Green peaks protruded high into the sky, as though they were pointing their way towards the gods in the heavens. Pepito felt a sense of calm come over him. Being in the wilderness was a welcome change from the stresses of the last two days. He clutched his bag tightly and continued to move along the undulating path.

The trail zig-zagged for several hundred feet as it continued to climb through the thicket of trees and short, prickly bushes. The dirt path soon gave way to gravel and Pepito became aware of the crushing sound beneath his feet. He was entering a higher elevation and the trail was becoming increasingly covered by the crumbling limestone rock that lined the sides of the path. Pepito kept a brisk pace – he knew he didn't have time to slow down or suffer a delay. Above him the crows began to caw loudly; he wasn't sure if they were searching for food or trying to communicate with him. Either way, he ignored them and continued to push on.

Thirty minutes passed. Pepito's thighs began to burn and his chest was feeling tighter and tighter. It was becoming harder to breath. Pepito was accustomed to running great distances at school, and he routinely left the rest of the team behind when doing wind sprints at soccer practice, but the thinner air at this elevation was affecting him. He forced the air in and out of his lungs with long, slow breaths. He wanted to stop and rest, but he knew he couldn't risk losing any time.

He continued to press on. The crumbled pebbles made the trail slippery and Pepito's old weathered sneakers didn't provide much in the way of traction. His feet slid out from underneath him and he had to be careful not to lose his balance and fall. "One foot in front of the other," he told himself, "just keep moving..."

After another ten minutes, the trail turned sharply to the left, and as he rounded the corner, Pepito noticed the trail led into a set of stone steps that ascended the hillside. Pepito sighed. He was already fatigued and now had to contend with this new challenge. He looked up; the stairway rose steeply above him and seemed never ending. He picked up his leg and stepped onto the well-worn stone step. "Maybe counting the steps will take my mind off the climb," he thought to himself. "One, two, three, four..." He finally stopped counting when he reached 39. He had reached the top. His heart was beating violently in his chest and he felt light headed and a little dizzy.

He looked around to survey his location. He was in the upper regions of the mountains. The sharp green and brown peaks shot up in all directions and they seemed to be covered by a layer of thick, soft carpet. Pepito stood in awe of the beauty around him. He clutched the bag; pride swelling inside for his land and the history of his people in these parts. After a few minutes, his breathing slowed down and his heart rate wasn't quite as rapid as before. It was time to get moving. He lowered his head and continued along the path.

The trail remained relatively flat for approximately 50 metres before Pepito encountered another staircase. This time the stone steps led downward into the bush below him. Pepito began his way down the limestone steps, "At least it's easier than going up," he thought. He counted again as he descended. He reached 29 before he stopped counting. "Things are getting easier..."

He stepped back onto the gravelly trail and slipped under the canopy of the forest. He felt optimistic about his position, "Maybe I reached the top of the trail and it's all downhill from here." He felt buoyed by the thought and strode forward with a quickened pace. He cut through several switchbacks before he stopped in his tracks.

Rising sharply in front of him was another staircase; this one seemed taller and steeper than the previous one. He felt his shoulders slump and he exhaled loudly in frustration. But he didn't have time to feel sorry for himself and he refused to be discouraged. Pepito once again lifted his foot, placed it on the stone step, and pushed down hard on his left thigh. As with the previous staircase, the stones had been eroded with use over time and there were noticeable depressions in the centre of each rock. As Pepito looked down, he wondered about all those people that had previously stepped on these same stones. This was the same path used by the original Shadow Runners, those that not only helped build the great Incan Empire, but also helped keep it a secret and protected from the invading Spanish soldiers. He wondered if they, too, felt the same pride as they climbed up and down the steps. The same steps that acted as a pipeline between the sacred home of Machu Picchu and the Incan community that surrounded it. He wondered too about all the people who walked this path bringing materials from Cusco to help build Machu Picchu. There must have been thousands of journeys by those who brought tools, food, and all sorts of other items needed to live in the sacred city. Then a thought struck Pepito, "If the Casa Del Oro was in Machu Picchu, then of course, the golden objects would have also made the journey along this path. These stones had seen not only the great people of his past, but the priceless treasures as well." Pepito felt empowered by his thoughts and continued to climb up the steep steps.

Although Pepito's resolve was strong, the trail continued to pose more challenges for him. The third staircase ended and reached a plateau, only to be met by another descending staircase 20 or so feet ahead. And then that staircase led to yet another one that climbed up once again to a higher elevation. Each staircase led, at varying distances, to another one that led in the opposite direction from the previous one.

This continued for some 15 minutes or so. Staircase after staircase. The trail was merciless at this stage and even though Pepito felt mentally tough, his body was showing signs of fatigue. His knees would shudder with pain with each step, particularly on the downhill steps as he tried to minimize the force of his entire weight coming down hard on them. He also began to feel some pain under his big toes and his heels. His shoes did not provide much support and he was sure that he would develop blisters before long. He was deterred but not broken and he grunted his way up the final steps of his current staircase, pushing his way through the pain. His grunting helped fuel his progress forward, but unfortunately, it prevented him from hearing the twig snapping in the trail behind him.

# CHAPTER 17

Senhor Gonzalez was busy grading tests in his office when he heard the doorbell ring. He put down his red pen and went to answer the door. He turned the tarnished brass knob and pulled open the door. For the second time in as many days, one of his students had presented themselves unannounced on his doorstep. Senhor Gonzalez smiled.

"Hello, Marta, how are you?"

"Hi Senhor Gonzalez, I'm fine... I'm sorry to bother you but I need your help."

"Yes, of course, what's the matter?" he asked.

"I'm... well... actually... it's Pepito," she said hesitantly.

Senhor Gonzalez' eyes narrowed and he inched closer to Marta. "What is it, Marta? What happened?" His voice was serious and filled with concern.

"He was in trouble... someone tried to take him. I'm not sure why. I think he's still in trouble and I'm worried about him," Marta said shakily.

"Do you know where he is?" asked Senhor Gonzalez.

"No, the last time I talked with him, he was with you."

"He came to me but left after a short visit..." Senhor Gonzalez voice trailed off as he recalled the conversation they had yesterday. Then he had a sudden revelation. "I think I know where he is!" Senhor Gonzalez looked down at his watch. It was 9:30am. "We don't have much time. We need to go right now."

"What's going on? Where is he?" pleaded Marta.

"We'll discuss everything on the drive," he said, gathering his keys and wallet. "We'll call your parents from the car, too." He rushed her towards the Toyota parked on the driveway. "We can't waste any time. We need to be there before twelve noon."

# CHAPTER 18

J ose pulled the truck into the parking lot of the train station at Ollantaytambo. Dust kicked up in the dry, dirt covered lot. He steered between two cars and slowed to a stop. He stepped out of the vehicle and surveyed the surroundings. A few people ambled about coming and going from the station. No one appeared suspicious or out of place.

For most visitors to Machu Picchu, the Ollantaytambo train station was a necessary stop. There were two options to get to the ruins from here: the train to Aguas Calientes (the nearest town to Machu Picchu) - which almost everyone took, or the rough backroads that zigzagged through a maze of valleys. These back roads were not signed and were used primarily by locals that lived in the area.

Jose headed towards the station and stepped inside. The train station was a small, single-room building consisting of three ticket windows, a convenience stand in the corner - where an older gentleman sat in a chair watching the passersby come and go - and two washrooms in the opposite corner.

Jose looked about the open space. A handful of people seemed to be going about their business – some buying tickets, others checking the schedules that lined the back wall. No sign of Cica or his gang. Jose strode outside to the platform. The boarding area was quiet with about a dozen people waiting for the next train to arrive. Some sat on benches while others stood or leaned against the light poles. Jose walked down the platform to get a look at the faces around him. He tried to look casual and unassuming as he examined the people. He didn't recognize a single person. Everyone appeared to be either a tourist, or a local on their way to work. Again, no one appeared suspicious. Jose stood on the platform and stared down the long train track as it progressed from the station and into the foothills nearby. He couldn't help but think that this path led not only to the ruins and Cica, but also to his son.

Jose wandered back into the main building. He scanned the station once again, examining all the people within. There was still one place he hadn't checked – the washrooms. He walked across the wooden floor and approached the white doors with the frosted glass windows. The paint was peeling around the edges of the window frames and the brass handle had been worn from years of use. Jose reached out to grab the handle when he felt his phone vibrating in his pocket. He pulled his phone out and saw the text from Rosita: "Javier called. Cica spotted by informant on P-ista de la Montagne."

Jose pushed the phone back into his pocket, dashed out of the train station, and sprinted towards the pick-up truck.

The country roads that wove around the mountains of Machu Picchu consisted of hard packed dirt and crisscrossed between farms and the occasional hamlet. Jose powered the truck up and around the undulating tracks.

"What exactly did Javier say?" he asked Rosita.

"A farmhand that he knows saw a strange car driving quickly along Pista de la Montagne just east of Pista Toltec," she answered. "He didn't rec-ognize the driver, but said that he was alone in the car."

"Did he give a description of the car?" asked Jose.

"A grey, older model four-door, maybe Jap-anese – Toyota or Nissan, but he wasn't sure," re-plied Rosita.

"He must have swapped the car in town with someone... might even be stolen... I'm sur-prised he came through these parts – wasn't aware he knew the roads here." Jose fell silent for a moment, pondering if Cica was perhaps shown these roads by Senhor Garcia in his efforts to train Cica for the job of Shadow Runner. Jose grit his teeth and exhaled sharply through his nose.

Rosita could sense Jose was becoming more enraged. She attempted to calm his nerves, "Well, at least it's just Cica on the move... it's a good thing that he didn't bring Alberto and Ramon... it will be easier to handle just one of them and not three," she offered.

Jose nodded.

Rosita continued, "Don't worry. We will catch up with Cica at the ruins – he'll probably head for the central square but he has nothing... no map... no indication of where to go... he most likely panicked waiting at home and is hoping to get lucky... he really has no clue. Don't worry, he has nothing. Everything will be alright."

Jose nodded again, the fire smoldering inside of him. He kept a firm grip on the steering wheel and a steely gaze on the path ahead. He continued to accelerate around the single lane road's twists and turns. The many blind corners posed a two-fold threat: no room to pass a slow-moving vehicle and no way to avoid colliding with an oncoming car. But this was no time to be cautious – time was at a premium. Jose's heart drummed violently as he continued to race along the narrow road kicking up clouds of dirt in his wake.

# CHAPTER 19

Pepito looked up at the sun. Its position was still slightly below the centre of the sky. Pepito guessed that it was probably close to, or just past, 11:00am. He had been moving steadily for about forty-five minutes and he figured that he was likely within two kilometres of Machu Picchu. The terrain had finally begun to level off somewhat and he hadn't seen a staircase in the past five minutes or so. He felt happy that his knees were given a reprieve from the pounding on the stairs.

The trail suddenly led out of the canopy and into an open area without any tree cover. The hot sun beat down on Pepito and for the first time he realized just how thirsty he was. He licked his dry lips and cursed himself for not having brought any water. He would give anything for even just a few sips at this point. But he couldn't feel sorry for himself. He could hold out for just a little while longer.

He lowered his head and continued to put one foot in front of the other. The trail did not stay flat for long and soon Pepito was walking towards the base of an exposed, rocky hillside. The trail narrowed and began to climb up the steep and gravelly path. As he climbed the trail, he became increasingly aware of how much the trail fell off on his left side. Pepito was always a little uncomfortable with heights and he could feel his legs buckle just slightly beneath him. He tried to direct his gaze on the path in front, but because the area was so exposed, the dramatic drop was always in view.

He tried to stay composed, "Just keep looking at the spot you want to go," he told himself. "You won't fall... you won't fall." He managed to fool himself for a few moments until suddenly he came across a small wooden bridge. Pepito stopped in his tracks and examined the bridge. It was about 20 feet long and only a few feet wide. There seemed to be a giant hole in the hillside – like an ice cream scoop carved out a chunk of the mountain. Mudslides were common in various parts of the Andes Mountains and sometimes entire roads would need to be closed when large sections slid down the mountainsides.

The feeble bridge was made of a series of loosely tied, narrow logs and spanned the gap left by the hole in the mountain. Pepito's eyes widened. There seemed like no other option. The cliff fell sharply below to his left and there was no way he could turn back now. There was only one route and that was across this bed of rickety looking tree branches.

He placed one foot on the edge of the bridge and gradually pushed down. To his surprise, the structure felt fairly stable. He decided to give it a shot. He placed his other foot on the bridge and stood standing for a moment to see if the logs could hold his weight. The bridge did not move. It felt secure despite its appearance. Pepito decided to take another step forward. His legs began to tremble and he felt his hands tingle. He did not dare look down at his feet or the sharp drop that began at the bridge's edge. Once again, his breathing became short and shallow – each breath he exhaled was charged with fear. "Look at where you want to go... it's just another part of the trail – just like the part before and after this... relax... stay calm, you can do it..." He took four or five steps, gingerly placing each foot in front of the other. He tried to be as light as possible, barely lifting his shoe above the wooden traverse. He seemed to be doing fine, and despite feeling a bit dizzy, he continued to walk forward slowly and steadily. He could feel the logs give ever so slightly beneath him and they creaked and moaned with each advancing step. "Stay calm... look ahead... you are half way there..."

Pepito took a deep breath. He had less than ten feet to go. He was nearly there. He took a step forward with his left foot when suddenly

it slipped over one of the logs and jammed itself into a small opening in the bridge. The force
pulled Pepito down hard on the logs. His left hand
and right knee slammed into the bridge while his
other hand waved frantically in the air, trying to
find something to hold on to. He quickly scrambled and managed to grab hold of one of the logs
with his left hand and steadied himself before
nearly losing his balance and tumbling over the
edge. He froze for a second, motionless, with two
hands and one knee on the bridge. His heart thundered in his chest. He looked down at his shoe and
saw it dangling in mid-air below the bridge.
Pepito adjusted his focus and looked downward.
The ground was at least 60 feet below – a fall at
this height would be disastrous. His head began to
spin and he could feel his stomach churning. He
closed his eyes. The wind whistled in his ears and a
crow, once again, cawed in the distance.

"You can do this... you can do this..." He
whispered to himself. He opened his eyes and directed his gaze at the well-worn running shoe suspended in the air. He was determined not to let
this bridge and the mudslide that created the gap
in the trail be what determined his fate. He would
not let that happen. He braced himself with both
hands and began to slowly lift his right knee upward, allowing his right foot to slide forward and
plant itself beneath him on the logs. He continued
to hold on tightly as he then pulled his left knee
upward as well. He felt his leg slide up between

the logs – his jeans scraping the bark on the logs. He continued until his shoe wedged against the underside of the bridge. He tried to pivot his foot so that it could slide through the opening as well, but the way he was positioned gave him little room to maneuver. "Think... think," he whispered. He thought of standing up and trying to force his foot through, but the thought of letting go of the logs with his foot trapped was too frightening. Pepito instead leaned forward and inched ever so slightly towards the bridge's edge. With his left leg now parallel with the bridge, he could rotate the ankle more freely. He twisted his foot sharply to the right and slowly eased the foot through and out of the opening. He exhaled loudly as his shoe dropped lightly on top of the logs. He was momentarily free.

Pepito ever so gently released his grip on the logs and began to lift himself back up to a standing position. He straightened up while simultaneously guiding the canvas bag behind his back. He stood tall with both feet firmly beneath him. He had been on the bridge long enough and decided to move forward. This time he looked down at the logs and inspected every spot before taking a step. He could see the ground ominously peering back at him between the logs, but he was not deterred this time. He was not concerned with what lay below, but rather, what lay ahead. He strode cautiously and keenly across the remaining section of the bridge. He triumphantly stepped off the bridge and back onto the safety of the gravel path. He then took a few more steps before stopping to turn back to look at what he had just conquered. A small smile appeared across his mouth, "You did it," he thought.

His moment of satisfaction, however, was soon interrupted when out of the corner of his eye he spotted something dark rustling in the distant forest below.

# CHAPTER 20

Rosita and Jose pulled up to the paved road that skirted the edge of Aguas Calientes, the closest town to Machu Picchu. Aguas Calientes was named after the hot springs that sprung from the nearby wells. The small town was frequented by visitors to the ruins and those seeking the medicinal benefits that a soak in the warm waters would provide. The town of less than two thousand people is surrounded on three sides by towering mountains, and despite its small size, serves as an important gateway to the holy city.

Rosita pulled out her phone and hit 'redial'. She listened as the phone rang repeatedly.

"Still no answer," she said turning towards Jose.

"Maybe he's still asleep," replied Jose. "He did have a stressful day yesterday..."

"I'll try again later... I'm sure he's okay..." said Rosita assuaging herself.

Jose turned onto the paved road and followed it for several kilometres as it ran along the southern border of town. Jose drove the truck cautiously over the railway lines that led to the A-guas Train Station and then turned into the adjacent parking lot that provided not only parking for the station, but also served as a meeting place for those taking the bus up the steep, switchback filled nine kilometre road to Machu Picchu's main entrance. Several tours buses and a few parked cars were scattered amongst the lot.

"I'm going to circle the lot, see if there is a car that matches the description," stated Jose.

"Cica might have parked in town – somewhere out of the way and taken one of the buses up the hill," said Rosita as she looked about the parking lot.

They encircled the lot without any sign of Cica or an older model grey car.

"Let's check the buses," said Jose as he pulled the truck up to the two parked mini buses.

The tour buses sat idling, waiting to fill up with more tourists. Rosita and Jose stepped out of the truck and approached the buses.

"Ola, good morning," offered Jose to the driver. "My wife and I are looking for our son – he's fourteen and we became separated this morning at the market... we are all going to Machu Picchu and thought maybe he came onto the bus to wait for us. Do you mind if we check to see if he's here?"

"No problem. Go ahead," replied the driver waving his hand towards the aisle.

"Thank you," said Jose as he stepped up into the bus and moved between the rows of seats.

Jose examined each section of seats, being careful not to appear suspicious. He passed a young Peruvian couple in the front, then a group of four female students, perhaps Americans on spring break, then on his right a middle-aged couple, again, they looked like out-of-country visitors. The travelers paid him no attention as he passed. Jose moved to the back of the bus and looked down at the last row of seats. They were empty. No one else was on this bus.

Jose turned and returned to the front of the bus. He thanked the bus driver again and stepped down on the ground where Rosita waited.

"Nothing," he said. "I'll try the other one," walking to the adjacent bus.

Jose repeated the process from the first bus but once again found no sign of Cica or his thugs on the bus. Jose felt both relieved and discouraged at the same time. He was hoping to avoid a scene on the bus in front of innocent strangers, but he was still faced with the uncertainty of Cica's where-abouts. Jose returned to Rosita again and let out a deep sigh. "Well, let's keep going," he said.

Rosita nodded. They strode quickly to-wards the truck and climbed inside. The engine roared to life and Jose pushed down hard on the gear shift. The tires spun as the truck charged towards the far end of the parking lot. The truck bounced onto the road at the base of the hill and began its ascent up the only road that connected the ancient ruins with the outside world.

# CHAPTER 21

Pepito stared at the distant cluster of trees and bushes. His eyes focused on the spot where he could have sworn he saw something. The sun was beating down hard and he was still a little woozy from the bridge crossing, but his gut told him that there was something or someone hiding behind the cover of green and brown leaves. He kept his gaze on the spot for several minutes, hoping to wait out whatever or whoever was being concealed. Pepito remained motionless. The bushes and trees, despite a light breeze passing overhead, did not move. The heartbeats in his chest ticked by as did the moments he had remaining to get to the ruins.

"Maybe it was nothing... maybe just my imagination," he tried to reassure himself. "I don't have much time... I have to keep going." Pepito wanted to turn and continue up the path but his instincts kept him grounded on the trail. He looked up; the sun was nearing the centre point in the sky – there wasn't much time left before the noon hour deadline.

Despite his hesitation, Pepito took a few steps backwards while he kept his sights set on the distant forest. There was still no movement coming from the suspicious spot. He slowly turned and faced the opposite direction – no time to waste now, he had to get to going. He clutched the bag and began to jog down the path as it descended from the edge of the hillside. He was happy to be leaving the steep face of the precarious hill but as he continued downward, he was no longer able to see the forest on the other side.

The trail soon flattened out and once again zig zagged its way into the forest canopy. Pepito kept a brisk pace as he cut through and around the bends in the trail. He occasionally looked back over his shoulder, but he couldn't see more than a few metres behind him. It appeared that no one was following him and he felt reassured that whatever he saw in the forest was probably a small creature, like a monkey or an olingo. Whatever it was, Pepito was sure that it wasn't coming after him. He kept his feet moving quickly, willing his body through this last part of the journey.

The trail suddenly opened into a meadow with patches of grass on either side. The grass seemed out of place to him after spending so much time on the mountainous trail. Pepito strode through the meadow as it slowly climbed up a short hill. Once at the top of the hill, he stopped to get his bearings.

He looked and saw that the meadow eventually gave way to the base of the hillside and the trail once again led into the forest. Pepito's gaze turned upward; the trail seemed to climb up the hillside and emerged from the forest at the top. He could make out a stone structure that stuck out from the top of the trees. He wasn't sure what the structure was, but he knew that he had to get there.

Pepito's focus was suddenly interrupted by the sound of voices. He looked down to his right and, to his surprise, noticed several people sitting on and around what appeared to be a small wooden bench at the edge of the meadow some fifty or so feet away. He was startled by their sight because he hadn't seen anyone on the trail until now and they looked like aliens dropped down mysteriously from above.

"Hello!" called out a middle-aged man wearing a blue coat and a big smile. Pepito looked across the group on the bench. It looked like a group of trekkers and their porters or guides. Beside the friendly man sat two other Peruvians – probably porters - leaning against three very large backpacks. Pepito had heard of porters that carried massive loads across the Inca Trail for tourists and suppliers, but he had never seen one before in person. Their stamina and strength was legendary among the people in Cusco. When children complained of doing chores around the house, parents often told them tales of porters who had carried hundreds of pounds of cargo on their backs for two days straight across the entire trail without stopping to eat, drink, or even sleep. "You think this is hard work? Try being a porter on the Inca Trail," was a common parental response.

The other four people consisted of a family of two parents and their two children, who looked somewhere between 9 and 12 years of age. Tourists were a common sight in Cusco and they usually fell within one of two main groups: the scruffy, young backpackers or the wealthier middle class families. The richer tourists were easy to spot because they often wore fancy, colourful outdoor sportswear. Pepito was always impressed with how their hiking boots all looked so new, like foreigners had a secret polish to keep their footwear looking clean and fresh.

The family with the guide and porters fell into the second group of tourists. They had blond hair and shiny metal walking sticks leaning against the makeshift bench. Pepito realized he hadn't said anything and they were all staring curiously at him. "Hello," Pepito finally managed while waving his hand cautiously in the air.

"We're almost there!" said the guide in the blue coat. Pepito nodded in agreement with him. "Where's your crew? Did you get tired of waiting for them?" the man asked chuckling.

"No... I... uh..." Pepito stammered. "They are... yes, behind me, but... yes... I got tired of waiting so I kept going..." Pepito felt bad for lying but he needed to avoid any delays or problems at this point.

"Well it's a perfect day to visit the ruins so it's understandable that you're anxious to get there," the man said as he took a sip from his glass bottled soda. Pepito swallowed hard and pressed his parched lips together.

"Do you have an extra drink that I could have?" he asked optimistically.

"Yeah, of course. Come on down," replied the man as he rummaged through a side pouch in one of the larger backpacks. "They aren't very cold anymore at this point, but at least it's still wet..."

"That's okay," said Pepito as he sprung down the downward side of the grassy meadow.

"Here you go," said the man as he handed Pepito a bottle of Inca Kola. Pepito thanked him and grabbed it from his hands. "Woah. Somebody's thirsty!" said the man reacting to Pepito's eagerness.

"Sorry," Pepito said sheepishly. He lifted the yellow soft drink to his mouth and drained nearly half the bottle in one sip. The familiar pineapple and bubble gum flavour mixture of Inca Kola never tasted so good. "Ahhh. That's good," said Pepito as he finished off the rest of the bottle.

"Do you want another?" asked the mother who, along with her family, seemed bewildered by Pepito.

"No... thank you, though. But I need to get going. I don't have much time."

"But what about your group? Aren't you going to wait for them?" asked the friendly guide.

"No, well... yes, but not here. I'm going to wait for them at the ruins. If you see them, please tell them that I went ahead and will wait for them at Machu Picchu." Once again, he felt terrible for lying to the friendly strangers, but he needed to get moving.

"Okay. We will. Safe travels. Maybe we'll see you there."

"Thanks for the drink... bye," said Pepito as he began walking away briskly from the group and back towards the trailhead at the entrance to the forest.

# CHAPTER 22

J ose and Rosita stood at the wooden security booth that was next to the concrete building that served as the main entrance gate. A long queue of visitors stood waiting anxiously to be let inside the ruins. Jose looked inside the open window and saw two security guards standing over a clipboard.

"Gentleman", he said, "could I have a word, please?"

The lean, older guard stepped towards Jose, "What can I do for you?" he asked.

Jose reached into his pocket and pulled out his wallet and flipped it open. He pulled out a military issued identification card and presented it to the guard.

"I'm Jose Capac – federal agent. National Security division. We need to get inside immediately," he said directly.

"What's going on? Something happen?" asked the security guard.

"We have a possible suspect on the premises. We've been following him and believe he is here. We need to get inside and get to him before he poses a threat."

"What kind of threat? Is he a suspect?" the guard asked narrowing his eyes.

"I can't disclose that information. Just inform your staff that we are here. Tell them to go about their usual duties - we will let you know if we need assistance," Jose said sharply.

"I need more information, I can't just -"

"Look there is no time to explain. We need to act now. If you want to check me out, have your supervisor call the President. He will tell you everything you need to know - do you understand? Now please excuse us, we have to get inside." Jose grabbed Rosita by the hand and the two of them stepped inside the security booth.

"Okay, fine," said the guard. "But I'm sending a guy to keep a close eye on you."

"Do what you have to," replied Jose as he and Rosita walked to the back of the booth. "Thanks for your cooperation," said Jose opening the rear door. They stepped out of the building and scrambled their way down the stone walkway that clung to the edge of the hillside. After a moment, the walkway turned left around the mountainside and ended at a passageway made of large rectangular stones. Rosita and Jose passed through the open doorway and stepped onto the sacred grounds of Machu Picchu. They stopped and looked at the grand sight before them. Although they had stood on that very spot before, the majesty of the towering green peaks still took their breath away.

# CHAPTER 23

Pepito darted up the trail once he reentered the forest. His legs sliced through the air. His stride was accelerated by the compart dirt on the trail and the soda in his bloodstream. He dashed upward and toward the distant clearing at the top of the hill approximately 500 metres away. He was racing against time and the sun that was now positioned nearly directly above him in the sky. He propelled himself forward, huffing and puffing as he sprinted up the remaining section. His legs burned but he blocked out the pain and kept driving forward. Just a few more strides and he would be there. "Fifty feet... twenty-five feet..." he said to himself.

Then his legs slowed – he had reached the top of the hill and the end of the trail. The trees ended and gave way to a large rectangular stone platform, like a giant stage atop the mountain. Pepito stepped out of the forest and onto the flat stone surface. He took a few steps forward. The stone floor was surrounded by a short, two-foot wall and at the far end of the platform was a narrow u-shaped entrance way, also made of stone.

He quickly realized where he was: the famous Sun Gate that marked the entrance to Machu Picchu. When he traveled to the ruins with his school, the teacher had pointed out the Sun Gate way off in the distance when they stood in the centre of Machu Picchu, but because of the steep drop that encircled the Gate, the young students were not permitted to go there. But now here he was at the hallowed site. Butterflies filled his stomach; he knew he stood at the precipice of his destination, as well as his destiny.

He charged ahead to the gate and then stopped once he was under the stone archway. He froze in his tracks. Lying before him was the magical site of Machu Picchu. It was a view that was so common and popular in Peru and beyond, but he had never personally witnessed the ruins from this vantage point. Below him sprawled the magical holy land of his people. Pepito drew a short, quick breath.

The ruins sat atop a flat portion of a peak that rises from the Urubamba Valley. In the centre of the flattened pinnacle was an inviting deep green, grassy field. Surrounding the field were rows of terraced houses and buildings – only the walls remained standing since the rooftops were made from thatch at the time. At the far edge of the field, the sugarloaf peak of Huayna Picchu

pointed majestically to the heavens.
site was enveloped by distant mounta
seemed to create a wall of protection fo
that hung in the clear Andean air. Pepito was overcome by its beauty. He swelled with pride and
his eyes watered. He let out a long, loud breath.
"Okay ... focus. This is it," he said to himself.

He reached down and lifted the flap on the
canvas bag. He looked down at the stone pieces
nestled in the bag. It was the first time he had
looked at the Clave since his mom sat him down
on the cot two days ago. Pepito suddenly became
very aware of his surroundings - he needed to keep
the Clave hidden from view. He looked around.
There were a few people clustered around the Sun
Gate and several more making their way up the
path from the ruins. They all looked like unassuming tourists going about their lives. They didn't
appear like any of Cica's people but he couldn't be
sure of anything right now. He needed to find a private spot to view the Clave and he needed to do
it quickly. He didn't have many options. He was in
plain sight and couldn't risk exposing the sacred
map.

Just as frustration was setting in, a group
of twelve or so Japanese tourists began walking
up the path from ruins up to the Sun Gate. "This
might be my best shot," thought Pepito. He waited
anxiously as the group ambled up the cobblestone
walkway to the base of the gate. Pepito moved to
the side of the path as the group assembled in

front of him. The group stopped to admire the magnificent view before them. They took turns posing for pictures and cooing over the site. Pepito snuck casually up alongside them and found a perfect buffer zone between the hillside and a group of three young women. He looked around one more time to make sure that he was out of sight, hidden from onlookers. Then, slowly and carefully, he lifted the stones out of the bag and placed them on the ground at his feet.

He kneeled down and lined up the four pieces in their proper order. He leaned back to get a better view of the map. He hadn't realized it before, but the map itself was the same view of Machu Picchu as from the Sun Gate. The map clearly showed the city in the clouds, Huayna Pic-chu, and the surrounding mountains. He thought back to what Senhor Gonzalez told him about the Circulo, "The map shows the altar where the Clave is to be placed..."

He examined the map closely. It looked like a crude drawing of the site. He could make out the central field and several rows of houses and build-ings but nothing stood out as a special marking. He continued to examine every inch of the image looking for a clue or anything unique, but he saw nothing. The picture looked almost too simple and ordinary. "What am I missing?" he thought. "Could it be that this isn't a real Clave? Or maybe the Clave doesn't really reveal the location of the Casa Del Oro." Pepito's pulse began to race. "Think.

Think!"

He started over, looking at the map once again from left to right and top to bottom. Once again, nothing stood out. "Maybe the thugs thought the same thing. Maybe they wanted the last piece so badly because the first three pieces didn't show anything. That must be it!" he suddenly realized. "The clue must be in the fourth piece – the one his mom kept hidden in the shed." Pepito focused directly on the fourth piece. The stone showed several rows of larger buildings that sat on the northern edge of the central field. The buildings then gave way to the rolling hillside that descended into the lower valley. Besides that, there wasn't much there on the stone's image. Pepito looked very closely at every line and detail on the fourth stone, but still couldn't find anything significant.

Pepito lifted his head back ever so slightly and that's when he saw it: a small half inch crack that ran from the hole in the centre of the Clave to the top of one of the buildings on the diagram on the fourth piece. Unlike other typical cracks in stone, this one was a perfectly straight line, as though it was made by a machine. The crack was no accident; it was too perfect to be a result of an accident. "This has to be it. This has to be the spot – the altar – where the Clave is supposed to go." Pepito was so relieved with his discovery that he didn't realize that his last statement was said aloud and had caught the attention of the three Japanese women standing near him. Pepito looked up and smiled sheepishly at them; he hoped they didn't understand him, or at the very least, didn't care what he was up to.

He looked down once again to the building at the edge of the crack. He had to figure out a way to find the altar once he was at the site. He noticed that the buildings on the map were clearer at the western end of the ruins – at the base of Huayna Picchu and blurrier as they moved towards the northern edge of the map. The simplest method would be to count the buildings from the northeast corner of the meadow, so he began to count: five to the right and eight buildings from the top. He repeated it out loud. "Five to the right and eight from the top..." Feeling confident, he slid the Circulo back in the bag and slung it over his shoulder. As he stood up, he realized more people in the group were looking at him curiously. Pepito smiled and nodded at the Japanese tourists, slipped the pieces back in the bag, then sidled away from them and down the cobblestone path that led to the ruins.

The bag bounced against his right hip as he darted downward. He was so anxious to reach the altar that his feet barely touched the uneven surface. As he approached, he could make out various clusters of people that were dispersed throughout the site, including a group surrounding a llama that stood on a terrace about fifty feet away. He was always bemused by tourists that were drawn to llamas, thinking them to be cute, exotic creatures but often finding out after getting spat on that they are quite short tempered and unfriendly to strangers.

Pepito looked down - the path began to curve in several S–shaped turns as it gradually levelled out over three stone terraces. Pepito instead jumped down on the grassy terraces to save time. He bounced over two ledges easily, but as he leapt over the last one, he came down hard on the grass. He tumbled forward and lost his footing – the bag slid over his shoulder and he rolled several times before bracing himself with his hands. He caught his breath, "Oh no, the Clave." He peered inside the bag – to his relief, the stones were not damaged. He picked himself up and looked directly ahead. He had reached the eastern edge of the meadow. The grassy pitch and surrounding buildings seemed so compact from the Sun Gate, but now he felt dwarfed by their size. The sun blazed overhead. He was running out of time. He grabbed the bag tightly and sprinted across the emerald field. The stone walls and the faces of the onlookers blurred past as he accelerated forward. He couldn't hear anything besides the beating in his chest and his harsh, short bursts of breath. He lengthened his stride and before he knew it, he was past the halfway point, "Keep going," he told himself, "almost there."

# CHAPTER 24

Rosita and Jose had fanned out and spent the better part of twenty minutes scouring the grounds looking for Cica. They checked all the rows of houses, altars, and communal buildings on the east and west sides of the central plaza. There was no sign of him. Jose and Rosita knew that there were endless hiding places in the nooks and crannies in the ruins, but if Cica was hoping to find the location of the Casa Del Oro, then surely he would be visible and not hiding in a concealed corner somewhere.

"Do you think he climbed Huayna Picchu?" asked Rosita. "It's possible that he's up there." The narrow path that climbed the sugar loaf peak of Huayna Picchu was dangerously sheer and not for the faint of heart.

"Maybe, but let's have a look at the Sun Gate first," replied Jose. "We can check out Huayna after that." Jose and Rosita dashed across the eastern edge of the central plaza and towards the multiple terraces of the south end. They ran for approximately 100 metres when suddenly Rosita stopped dead in her tracks and grabbed Jose by the arm. She pulled the two them towards the stone wall that lined the grass field. "Wait, hide!" she hissed. She then darted inside the nearest doorway still clutching Jose by the arm. The two of them stopped and caught their breath.

"I saw him. He's just over there by the far wall," said Rosita anxiously.

Jose peered out slowly from behind the doorway. He inched his face forward until he could see the terraces at the south end of the field – the same terraces that marked the ascent to the Sun Gate. He took a short, sharp breath. There, with his back flat against the six-foot high stone terrace, stood Cica. Jose could barely make out the familiar snarl on his face, but that was surely him, standing there with his head cocked and arms at his side, waiting to pounce.

"Wait here," said Jose. "I'm going to drop down on the lower level and sneak up beside him."

Rosita looked worried, she didn't like how exposed they were. Things could get out of control and there were so many innocent people around.

"Be careful," she whispered.

"You too," Jose whispered back. He then turned and disappeared into the maze of passageways.

Rosita watched him go and then peered out slowly into the central plaza. Her body trembled when she caught sight of Cica. She breathed in deeply as her heart thumped loudly in her chest. "What is he doing?" she thought. "What is he waiting for?" Cica continued to stand rigidly with his back pushed hard against the wall. He seemed to be hiding from something or someone on the Sun Gate side of the plaza, but the few people that were on the path were much too far away for Rosita to make them out. "What is he up to?" she wondered aloud trying to keep her body from shaking. The seconds ticked by like an eternity. Rosita wanted so badly to confront Cica and put an end to her misery, but she had to wait for Jose to make his move. She bit down hard on her lip and breathed sharply through her nose.

After a brief moment, she saw Jose emerge from the lower terrace that was about 30 feet from Cica's right side. Cica's head was still cocked to the left and he didn't see Jose lift himself onto the main field. Rosita covered her mouth with her hand. Jose was in a crouch. He reached into the holster that sat in his lower back and pulled out his .357 Derringer pistol. He slid his finger over the trigger and slowly inched towards Cica. Jose remained in a crouched position as he continued to get closer and closer to his nemesis. Rosita could barely breath and her body shook violently. Jose continued to step closer. He was now some twenty feet away when a nearby woman shouted, "Gun!"

Cica's head turned quickly to his right. He

spotted Jose. Jose stopped advancing, stood up tall, and ordered Cica to put his hands in the air. Cica smiled menacingly and shook his head from side to side.

"Well if it isn't Jose Capac himself..." he said disdainfully.

"Don't make a scene here, Cica," ordered Jose. "We can do this the easy way... you, and no one else gets hurt."

"Easy way, huh?" Cica retorted. "We are long past easy." Cica put his hands in the air and then started to slowly move towards Jose.

"Stop, Cica. Don't move any closer," directed Jose, pointing his gun directly at Cica.

Cica continued to advance, "What are you going to do? Shoot me right here, in front of all these people?" He continued to move ever closer to Jose.

"Jose!" Rosita yelled out. But just as she did, Cica bent down and lunged at Jose. Jose attempted to fire the gun but Cica knocked the gun out his hands as he dove towards his midsection. Cica crashed into Jose and the two of them fell to the ground. They stumbled several steps backwards before they were able to pick themselves up again. They stopped and stared at one another. The gun lay several feet behind Cica. Just as Jose began to lung forward, Cica once again shot towards Jose's stomach and tackled him down to the ground again. This time they held onto each other, wrestling towards the edge of the terrace below.

Rosita yelled out again, "Jose, no!" but it was to no avail. Jose and Cica fell off the edge of the grass and dove headlong into the terrace one story below.

# CHAPTER 25

C ruz and Castillo stood at the top of the Sun Gate looking down at the scene below. They had last seen Pepito as he sprinted the length of the field but now he was hidden from view in the maze of the site's stone structures.

"Let's go. We got to stay close to him," stated Cruz.

"Maybe we should try calling again," offered Castillo.

The two junior thugs had followed Pepito from a distance along his entire journey on the Inca Trail. They were careful to remain out of sight. Cica's instructions to them were clear: "Follow him, don't let him know you are there, and call me every 15 minutes with your status."

Cruz and Castillo were able to make good on two of the three. Shortly after entering the trail, they lost their cell phone signal, and despite the occasional bar on their screen, were unable to send or receive any calls. They stayed within 100 metres or so and kept a close watch on Pepito's actions. The cat and mouse game played out for the most part of the 5 kilometre trek.

They were tempted to charge at him and steal the bag when he was stuck on the bridge, but he managed to release himself before they could pounce. When Pepito stopped on the other side of the bridge and stared at them, they were convinced that they had blown their cover. Luckily, the spot they were hiding in was protected by thick forest and shadow cover. Their close call forced them to hang back further and allow more time and distance between themselves and their mark.

Now they were uncertain of what to do next. They were not sure what would be worse: losing Pepito or having to deal with Cica's wrath. After a brief back and forth, they decided to call Cica and get further instructions. Cruz hesitantly took out his phone, he had a weak but visible signal. He punched in the numbers and held the phone to his ear. He winced with every ring, fearing the sound of Cica's imminent voice. The phone rang several times but with no answer. Cruz let the phone ring several more times but still no answer. Cruz shook his head. "He's not answering." He clicked to end the call.

"Now what do we do?" asked Castillo.

"We have no choice... let's get down there and find that kid."

# CHAPTER 26

Cica, having avoided any injury from the fall, scrambled over to Jose. Jose was lying still on the stone terrace, a small pool of blood leaked onto the rock below his head. Cica brought his face closer to Jose. Cica could see that he was still alive, barely breathing, but still alive. He could hear voices approaching from the level above, so he picked himself up and darted into the nearest building. He weaved in and out of several rooms before hiding behind a small concealed corner tucked away from any tourists.

Cica pulled out his phone, saw he had a missed call, and called Cruz. The phone only rang once.

"Boss," answered Cruz.

"Where are you? Where's the kid?" whispered Cica.

"We're coming down from the Sun Gate, almost at the central plaza."

"And the kid?" asked Cica sharply.

"Well... he... uh... we... kind of lost sight of

him..." answered Cruz hesitantly.

Cica clenched his mouth tightly, "What do you mean you lost sight of him?"

"We were right behind him, but once we got here he mixed in with the crowds and we couldn't see which way he went..." explained Cruz.

Cica was smoldering with fury. "When I finish with that kid, I'm going to pummel the both of you – you got that!"

"Yeah, yeah, sorry boss... don't worry... we'll find him."

"You better! And don't call me until you have something good to tell me. You and that other monkey, got that?" Cica said furiously. He pressed down on the phone, ended the call, and shoved the phone into his back pocket. Cica took a short, sharp breath. "That kid is around here somewhere," he thought to himself, "it's time to find him and get what's mine." Cica stepped out of the alcove and made his way through the maze of passageways on the western side of the ruins.

Rosita watched in shock as both men disappeared from view over the edge of the field. Rosita sprinted over to the corner of the field, snatched up the gun and dashed over to the terrace. She stopped at the edge and looked down. She gasped loudly. On the grass below, Jose lay unconscious – a trickle of blood fell from his left temple. Urgently, she looked around. Cica was gone. Jose was the only one on the terrace below. "Oh my god," she thought, "Oh my god..."

Rosita stuffed the pistol in her back pocket and began climbing down the exposed stones that acted as a staircase between the two different levels. She landed on the lower grassy field and raced towards Jose. She knelt down and cupped Jose's head in her hands. "Please wake up, my love... please wake up." she said shakily. Jose remained unconscious. She could see his chest rising ever so slightly as he gently breathed in and out. "Jose... Jose... it's me... come on... please wake up..." said Rosita choking back tears. "I need you... Jose... we need you..." She couldn't hold back any longer and her body began to shake, tears streamed down her face and she began to sob.

As if sensing her pain, Jose's eyelids began to flutter and after a brief moment, they lifted open. He was awake. "Hey... it's okay..." he whispered quietly.

Rosita's eyes met with his, "Jose! My love – oh thank God!" she said excitedly. "I was so worried..." Jose breathed in deeply and a small smile formed in the corners of his mouth. "Are you okay?" asked Rosita. "Are you hurt?"

Jose took another deep breath and exhaled slowly, "I'm okay. Don't think anything is broken... my head is pounding... but that's about it..."

Before Rosita could respond, a voice called out from overhead.

"Is he alright?" Two security guards were standing on the upper level above Jose and Rosita.

"He has a head injury. We need medical assistance," Rosita answered.

"I'll call for an ambulance," said the guard pulling out his phone.

Rosita looked back down at Jose. He squinted his eyes to protect his throbbing head from the sun's glare. "It's going to be okay," comforted Rosita, "help is coming... it's going to be okay..."

Unbeknownst to Rosita, some 80 feet away on the upper level, Pepito dashed across the emerald grass of the central plaza with the canvas bag held tightly beside him.

# CHAPTER 27

Pepito slowed down once he approached the western end of the field. He looked to his right and spotted the path that marked the building's perimeter. He cut hard to his right and hopped onto the cobblestone walkway. He took a deep breath and slowed down once more to concentrate on counting the buildings. Each row was marked by a narrow lane that ran perpendicular to his path. He counted as he went along, "one, two, three..." He stopped once he reached the fifth row. Again, he turned right and counted each of the buildings on the south side. There was no gap between the structures, but an open doorway marked the end of one home and the beginning of another. He called out each number as he went along. He remembered from his earlier visit that the guide described this area as the main residence of the priests and nobility. The homes in this section were larger than the others in Machu Picchu.

Finally, he arrived at the eighth house.

He stepped through the doorway and into a vast, empty room. He looked around. The three walls surrounding the doorway were approximately nine feet high, perfectly solid and level at the top. The fourth wall, the one opposite door and facing south, was quite different. Running about three feet above the ground was a stone ledge that ran across the back wall. It was about a foot wide and one foot thick. Pepito looked at the ledge and then tilted his gaze upward. The top of the wall looked odd. Instead of a flat surface, the wall had numerous curved, almost semicircled shaped stones spread across the top. The pattern seemed to be: two flat stones followed by one curved stone. He counted the curved stones – there were 19 in all. "One of those stones must be the altar. The Clave must sit on top of the curved part," thought Pepito. "One of those stones...but... which one?"

He began to panic. "Time is running out... which stone is it? Should I try every one of them and see?" His hands began to tremble. "I don't have time... and I could be wrong... think... think... what would make sense... what would his ancestors..." Pepito began to think back to his history lessons with Senhor Gonzalez. "Was there something he said that might help now?" Pepito recalled his teacher's lessons about sacrifice and primitive ball games and how they used the large rock quarry to build the structures... but nothing seemed to help him. "How do I know which number it is... numbers... what numbers..." Then it struck him: the quipo!

The quipo was a technique used by the Incas to record numbers and store materials – an ancient filing system of sorts. Most young Peruvian students are told of the system in math, not history class. The quipo is a sequence of three numbers: five, eight, six. The sequence helped with the organizing of materials and information.

Pepito thought back to his initial count: "There were five rows of buildings and eight houses, just like the quipo! The altar must be the $6^{th}$ stone!" He counted the $6^{th}$ stone starting at the north-west corner of the room. Once he spotted his target, he scrambled forward to the ledge and jumped on top. He paused for a moment. "What if it isn't the quipo- what if it's just a coincidence that I started counting from that corner? What if I'm wrong?" Pepito was suddenly filled with doubt. "It could be any of these altars, really." Just as Pepito was resigned to start over, he remembered the total count of all the curved stones on the top of the wall: 19 stones. Nineteen is the sum of the three numbers in the quipo. "That can't be a coincidence... this must be it."

With renewed confidence, Pepito flipped open the bag and pulled out the two lower pieces of the Clave Circulo. He reached up and slid the two pieces into the cradle of the curved stone. It fit like a glove. Pepito then scampered back down and pulled the other two pieces from the bag. Once again he slid with his body up along the wall trying desperately to fit the upper stones on top. He reached up as far as he could. The Clave pieces clung perilously between his thumbs and forefingers. He extended his whole body as much as possible – his feet barely touching the ledge at this point. He reached upward. Finally, he could feel the two pieces reach the top of the anchored pieces. They were sitting ever so slightly on the edge. Pepito gingerly pushed them forward. He was careful not to push too hard otherwise the top pieces would tumble down the other side of the wall. Pepito's fingers trembled, but he continued to slide the stones slowly and delicately forward. It felt that he was standing on the ledge for hours, but only seconds had passed. He continued to slide until finally he felt the top pieces become flush with the bottom ones. The Clave was in place. Pepito could barely contain his excitement. He stepped down on ledge, leaned back and looked up. There on top of the wall, a beaming laser of glorious orange light shot directly through the opening in the Clave Circulo.

# CHAPTER 28

The sun shone through the centre of the Circle Key like a heavenly flashlight. Pepito lifted himself up on the ledge and craned his neck to get a better look. The rough edges of the inner circles created a series of random shadows on the edge of the solar spotlight. Pepito looked around the perimeter of the spotlight for a clear or specific marking and searched for a moment before seeing it. There on the northeast edge of the spotlight was a distinctive sinuous black shadow. It looked like a slender snake crawling along the far end of the central field; a slithering arrow pointing the way to the treasure.

Pepito followed the shadow from the tail, up its body, and to the head. He narrowed his eyes to see exactly what the head was pointing towards, or at the very least, what lay in the surrounding area. The head of the snake appeared to be hovering over the famous Intihuatana Stone. The stone was a sacred location within Machu Picchu. It was massive, several feet long and across, placed on the western end of the ruins and each of its corners pointed directly to the four cardinal directions. It served as a prehistoric compass providing a very exact understanding of where north, south, east, and west lay in the context of the holy city. It was a compulsory stop for most school trips to Machu Picchu and certainly a well-known landmark for anyone who has been to the ruins.

The mouth of the serpentine shadow seemed to be just below the northern corner of the Intihuatana Stone. Pepito wasn't sure what to make of this sighting. The head of the snake appeared to be pointing to the northern corner but it was not directly beside it, instead the mouth seemed to be falling away from the corner and the rest of the famous rock.

"Maybe it's pointing to something else," thought Pepito. "Maybe I have to wait to see if it will point to another spot nearby." He looked around the vicinity of the head to see if he could make out another obvious location. He scanned the area surrounding the serpent's head. Cobblestones covered the platform area where the Intihuatana Stone stood, but they were much too small in relation to the shadow's mouth to indicate if one stone was the secret location. Pepito became increasingly frustrated and discouraged – there wasn't much time – the sun would dip soon and he would lose any chance of seeing the light through the inner circle.

"There's no time to waste," he said to himself. "There is no time to waste... wait... time! The time. That's it. The time must be past noon." He looked up at the sky to get a bearing on the sun's location above, but the blinding light forced him to immediately shut his eyes. "It must be after noon," he told himself again reassuringly. "The mouth is moving away from the corner because at twelve o'clock it pointed exactly at the corner." Pepito was brimming with excitement. "That has to be it," he whispered aloud. "The corner must point to where the Casa is located." Pepito reached up and gathered the four pieces of the Clave and placed them gently in the canvas bag. He cautiously stepped down from the ledge and slung the bag over his shoulder. Pepito had two thoughts ricocheting through his head: "Get across the central plaza and over to the Intihuatana Stone," and "don't let anyone see you do it."

Pepito managed to slink his way through a series of openings and walkways that skirted the central plaza and emerged on the western side of the ruins where the Intihuatana Stone sat like a stoic beacon. He stood in an entranceway that was about 30 feet from the Stone. He scanned the platform for anyone or anything suspicious. But, like in most other parts of the site, there were only a handful of tourists posing and taking photos, and a tour guide orating the Stone's history and purpose.

Pepito felt safe and ventured slowly towards the Stone's northern corner. He tried to appear casual and relaxed, but all the while he kept a vigilant eye out for any potential thugs. He took a few more steps and finally arrived at the rock's northern apex. "The legend says that the snake points to the spot where you begin the path to the Casa," Pepito thought to himself. "So, the corner must also point to where the path begins." Pepito stood with his back to the northern corner of the Stone and looked directly at the area in front of him. He spotted Mount Salcantay, one of the sacred peaks that lay on the outer border of the ruins. The famous mountain was nearly directly in line with where he stood. Pepito then looked down and saw that just a few feet below him, a series of steps descended from the platform from where he stood and into the valley at the base of Machu Picchu. He continued to track the stairs as they ended at the bottom of the hill and led into a dirt trail that disappeared into the forest below.

Pepito's heart began to race. He instantly recalled what the guide told to his class during the school trip: "Intihuatana Stone not only points to a precise cardinal direction, but there is a path that leads from each corner of the stone and follows to the exact location of that direction in the hills nearby." Pepito shook with elation. "This trail leads to the north and it ends on the side of that mountain... wherever this trail ends – that's where the Casa Del Oro is." Pepito darted down the rocky steps and toward the trailhead below.

# CHAPTER 29

The train rolled to a stop at the Machu Picchu station in Aguas Calientes; a loud horn announced its arrival. Marta and Senhor Gonzalez followed the crowd out of the train and down onto the platform below. The passengers scattered in both directions, and Marta and Senhor Gonzalez stopped to take in their surroundings. Unlike standard stations, the one in Aguas Calientes stopped in the middle of town on a typical street lined with food stalls and small shops. Once you disembarked the train, there was no need to exit the station – the town began at the edge of the tracks.

"I'm going to ask in here," said Senhor Gonzalez motioning towards a narrow coffee shop directly in front of them. Senhor Gonzalez stepped forward and maneuvered between the two white plastic chairs that sat by the café's windows. Marta followed him in and the two of them approached the young, slender employee behind the counter.

"Hello," said Senhor Gonzalez.

"Hi, what can I get you?" asked the server.

"Actually, I just need some help... can you please tell me where the police station is?" The server looked curiously at Senhor Gonzalez and then at Marta who stood just behind his right shoulder. "Don't worry – it's nothing to worry about – we just need to possibly file a report... a minor report," said Senhor Gonzalez reassuringly.

The employee wasn't sure what to make of the request but felt the stranger and young girl looked harmless enough. "Just go right outside the shop, and continue until you see the big market – the artist market. Pass through the market until you get to the big square on the far side. From there you will see the police station in the opposite corner of the square."

"Thank you. Thank you very much," replied Senhor Gonzalez as he turned to face Marta.

"Are you sure we should go there and not Machu Picchu instead?" asked Marta, still not convinced that this was the right course of action.

"It's well past 12 noon so we don't even know if Pepito is anywhere near the ruins," replied Senhor Gonzalez. "And remember, if Pepito is in any real danger, then we have to contact the police."

Marta sighed deeply, "Okay, I guess that's the right thing to do."

"Come on, let's get going," said Senhor Gonzalez, and the two of them headed out the café and west on Avenida Hermanos Ayar.

# CHAPTER 30

Pepito jumped down the final stone step on the staircase that led down from the upper portion of the ruins down to the forest in the lower valley. He stopped and looked down the dirt trail that lay ahead of him. He spun around, tilted his head upward and peered at the wall of stone that he had just descended. The layers of the narrowing floors seemed to be pointing directly into the heavens. Pepito, sensing that no one had seen him, felt safe and secure that he was alone.

He turned again and faced the trailhead at the entrance to the forest. He took a deep breath and stepped forward. The trail was narrow, barely a foot across, and littered with small stones and tree roots. While the trail was known by many, few traveled along it, and its lack of use was apparent. Pepito strode forward. The trees and bushes encroached the trail both on the sides and overhead – as Pepito moved along, he frequently ducked down to avoid hitting the low hanging branches. The trail, however, was nearly a perfectly straight line, cutting a direct path through the valley to the base of the nearby mountain.

Pepito quickened his pace and began to dart through and around the overgrown bushes. His legs were tired from the previous hike, but now he was galvanized by the thought that the Casa Del Oro was only a few moments away. He pressed on and continued to dance over the obstacles on the trail. "Almost there," he told himself. "Almost there."

Just over ten minutes later, Pepito saw a small clearing up ahead. Sunlight from above illuminated a circular opening in the trail. Pepito's pulse quickened and he charged ahead, floating over the last few metres of the trail.

He arrived at the clearing and came to a full stop. The trail ended at the base of the steep hillside. Pepito stared straight ahead. His eyes widened. There in front of him was a large pile of crumbled stones. The debris was several feet high and across – a clump of broken stones in different shapes and sizes. It looked like someone had taken a sledgehammer to a giant wall and knocked every last stone out of place.

Pepito moved closer to get a better look. The pile of rubble was bigger than he thought – it extended for several metres in front of the hillside. As he moved to the side, Pepito could see the stones were perhaps blocking an entrance, but it would take him forever to clear the pile, and some stones were far too big for him to lift by himself. Pepito sighed with disappointment. "This must be the entrance to the Casa..." he thought to himself. "Or maybe it was the old entrance..." He recalled what Senhor Gonzalez said about the location of the Casa and how people believed that it had been moved from its original location.

"Maybe this was where the Casa used to be... whoever did this probably moved the treasures and smashed the entrance..." There was no way to be sure. Pepito shook his head in despair. "What should I do?" he thought. "What should I do?" Pepito moved back to the front of the large mound of rocks. He scanned the forest above the debris. Nothing there. He then moved to the other side of the pile and moved closer to the spot where the rock met the bushes on the hillside. He scanned the area closely. Again, nothing there. Pepito began to grit his teeth in frustration. "This can't be the end – there must be something here." He continued to peer closely and then suddenly something caught his eye.

Directly above the pile, he spotted something shiny amongst the thorny bushes. Pepito nearly jumped with excitement. He scrambled up the rock pile, reached the top and began to push aside the branches that concealed the mysterious object. It was letters, something was written on a plaque or another large rock. He pushed away the branches – he could see it now in its entirety: an inscription written on a single, large rock inserted in the hillside. The letters were carved into the stone, but clearly legible. They read:

> **O**riginal **R**eligious **O**ffering
> a **L**argess of **E**steem and **D**evotion to
> **A S**hrine in **A**guas **C**alientes

Pepito stared at the quotation for quite some time, pensively pondering its meaning. "What was the offering? Is this place an offering? What is a 'largess'?" It didn't make any sense. "A shrine in Aguas Calientes? I don't know of any shrine there... maybe a church... Original offering? I know that the ancients would offer valuable stuff to the gods, but what did they offer? The gold? Maybe..." Pepito continued to contemplate the message in the inscription, but he was left with many questions and no answers. He sat down on the top row of stones and continued to examine each word.

He stared closely at the statement, and then in an instant, he noticed something odd. "Each of the main words are capitalized," he thought. "And the small words are not capitalized except for the 'A' in the last line... why is that word capitalized when the others aren't?" he asked himself. Pepito leaned forward, narrowing his vision. The capital letters appeared slightly thicker than the other letters. "There must be something to this..." Then he saw it. "The first row... the first letter of each word spells ORO – gold!" He looked down at the second row. "L.E.D." He whispered. "What is LED? LED..." He bit down on his lip. "LED... LED... wait. Not LED, it's backwards: DEL." He quickly scanned the bottom row. "ASAC. It's backwards. It's CASA! All the letters are backwards: CASA DEL ORO!" Pepito jumped from the stone and nearly lost his balance. "Yes!" he exclaimed, pumping his fist in the air. "That's it! The Casa Del Oro is in a shrine in Aguas Calientes. Pepito scrambled down from the stone pile and leapt onto the ground below. He clutched the canvas bag securely at his side and bolted down the path back to Machu Pic-chu.

# CHAPTER 31

Pepito emerged from the central doorway that led into the ruins. He stepped through the stone archway and onto the path that led back to the main ticket booth. He had a vague recollection of the layout of the entrance, but he knew that this route would take him back to the parking lot where the buses waited to take visitors back into the town of Aguas Calientes.

He walked briskly with anticipation, and even though his stomach growled from hunger, his legs carried him forward with ease. Pepito rounded the final corner of the path and came upon the cluster of tourists surrounding the main entrance. As he pushed through the crowd and past the exit turnstile, he noticed a small crowd was gathering in a corner of the parking lot. He moved closer to get a better look – he quickly noticed an ambulance was parked by the curb and people were busily gesturing and chatting around it.

"I wonder what's going on?" Pepito thought

to himself. "Looks like someone needs help... probably some old person overdid it trying to climb up all the staircases... hope they're okay..." Pepito did not have time to worry about the ambulance and why it was there – he had more pressing issues like where the buses were. He scanned the parking lot. At the far end of the lot he spotted a shuttle bus rolling slowly backwards from a parking spot. Pepito held tight to the canvas bag at his side and bolted for the bus. Within a few seconds he was streaking at top speed across the narrow parking lot.

The driver of the shuttle bus came to a full stop, slid the gear shift into 'drive' and then turned the wheel several times to his right as the bus began to roll forward. Pepito accelerated ahead – his legs slicing through the air. The bag began to bounce on his hip, but Pepito continued to sprint towards the bus. "Hey! Wait!" he yelled out, but the bus continued to advance and was gaining more speed. "Wait!" he yelled again, but the driver continued ahead. Pepito grunted loudly and raced up to the bus – he was now only a few metres away. His burning legs kept charging ahead. Only a few feet away now – the bus was practically within reach. "Hey!" he yelled again. Suddenly a passenger in the back seat turned and looked out the rear window. They had spotted Pepito. The passenger called out to the driver and within a few moments the bus was slowing down. Pepito, relieved, slowed down and moved along the side of the bus towards the door. The bus came to a stop and the door swung open with a hiss. Pepito stood hunched over, panting hard. The bus driver peered at him quizzically. Pepito looked up and smiled. He took two short, quick breaths, "Do you have room for one more?" he asked. The bus driver nodded and Pepito dragged himself up the steps and onto the bus.

Two hundred metres away, Cruz and Castillo rushed towards the ruins' exit. They had been walking back to the main entrance, frustrated by not having found Pepito, when they suddenly heard him yell out in the parking lot. They tried squeezing through the throng of people but were unable to make it out to the parking lot before the shuttle bus drove out of sight.

"Dammit!" said Castillo. "I can't believe this kid's luck..."

"I'm calling Cica," replied Cruz taking out his cell phone. Cruz hit 'redial' and brought the phone close to his ear. "Hey Boss. We saw him... he's on the bus – heading down the road... the one that goes back to town."

Cica responded tersely, "Do not let him out of your sight. I'm on my way to Aguas."

Cruz tried to reply but the Cica had already hung up.

# CHAPTER 32

Senhor Gonzalez and Marta had been sitting patiently in the police station lobby for over twenty minutes. They sat in a corner on two old office chairs with the seat cushion poking out in the corners. A small fan hissed in the corner. Marta tapped at her thigh, growing anxious with each passing minute.

"Don't worry," offered Senhor Gonzalez, "they will be with us soon..." He tried to smile and comfort Marta but he sensed that she was growing uneasy with worry.

Just then, a young, slim police officer stepped from behind the counter and into the lobby. His uniform looked clean and new – and slightly too big for his slender frame.

"Hello. Sorry to keep you waiting," the officer said reaching his hand out to Senhor Gonzalez. He seemed nervous and unsure of himself. "I'm Officer Nunes... sorry for the delay... we have been very busy today with the parade – and we had a fight, well two guys got into a fight at Machu Picchu and... anyway... what can I do for you?"

Senhor Gonzalez sighed deeply, "Well, we need your assistance. There is something we need to tell you." He turned to Marta, "Are you ready?"

Marta nodded assuredly.

"Go ahead," he said encouragingly.

Marta turned to the novice officer and began, "it all started two nights ago when my friend Pepito and I were in Plaza de Armas in Cusco..."

# CHAPTER 33

Pepito stepped off the shuttle bus and into the bright sun that washed over the gravel parking lot. He thanked and said good bye to the kind stranger that he sat next to at the front of the bus. The elderly man worked as a part time tour guide at the ruins, and not only did he entertain the passengers on the bus by playing the wooden flute, but he also helped direct Pepito to the exact location of the church in Aguas Calientes.

The elderly man waved good bye and Pepito set off in the opposite direction. Just a few blocks and a few anxious minutes separated him from his destination. "Two blocks up along the river and then turn right... Then follow that street to the main square in town..." he repeated to himself.

Pepito looked around to take in his surroundings. He marveled at how picturesque the town was with rows of brightly colored stores that lined the narrow, serpentine streets. He looked up and panned the area – the entire town seemed enveloped by the lush, green hills of the Sacred Valley.

At this point, he made it to Avenida Contisuyo, and turned right. "The main square and the church are at the end... just follow the street to the end," he reminded himself. The wide avenue was lively and abuzz with weekend tourists and locals decorating their storefronts for the upcoming parade. Pepito kept moving past the crowds and food vendors. After a few minutes, the stalls ended and the street narrowed, turning more residential. The food vendors quickly gave way to apartment doors and windows with colourful-flower boxes. Pepito continued down the road, moving swiftly through the less busy part of the avenue.

A moment later, he saw the narrow street open up into the main plaza. Once again, the sun provided a bright spotlight for the open square and the buildings surrounding it. Pepito moved to the edge of the plaza and scanned from left to right. The square was not empty as most people had made their way to the riverside for the parade.

It didn't take long before Pepito spotted the humble grey stone church on the far side. He took a deep breath and swallowed hard. "There it is," he thought to himself. He took a step forward and then stopped himself abruptly.

He was suddenly distracted by the large, bronze statue that stood squarely in the centre of the plaza. It was a statue of a proud warrior standing with one foot in front of the other, arms outstretched and one hand holding a tall spear with a large arrowhead at the tip. The statue wore a headdress with three pointy leaves and a circular medallion in the centre of his forehead. Pepito knew this image and person well. It was a statue of Pachacutec - one of the greatest Incan emperors of all time. Pepito was well versed on his story. Senhor Gonzalez often spoke of Pachacutec's accomplishments and his importance to Incan history. He was known for his bravery and loyalty, but his greatest legacy is that he ordered the construction of Machu Picchu. His vision and passion are the reasons why the holy city exists today. Pepito had forgotten about the Pachacutec statue, but there it was now shining brightly in the afternoon sun. He stepped forward and hurriedly made his way to the foot of the statue.

The statue stood on a large square shaped platform of stacked stones. The platform was approximately five feet high and nearly 50 feet long and 50 feet wide. The platform was bordered by a shallow moat that caught the pouring water from the four fountains that sat prominently in the centre of the structure's four sides. The statue was an imposing presence at over ten feet tall from head to toe. Pachacutec's face was intense yet sympathetic, and his mouth was slightly agape – as though he had a secret he wanted to share. His open arms displayed a feeling of acceptance, but the long, pointed spear in his right hand also warned enemies that he was not to be messed with.

Pepito stood underneath him and gazed up in wonder. Once again, Pepito felt strongly connected to his people and their storied history. His eyes squinted under the glare bouncing from the tip of the spear. Pepito looked away to protect his eyes and caught sight of the church that sat in the background behind Pachacutec. Suddenly, he remembered why he was there in the first place – the church. He clutched the canvas bag and strode to the modest house of worship.

Pepito stepped up the two steps towards the church and approached the large brown wooden door. He reached out, grabbed the tarnished knob, turned it to the right and pushed. The door did not budge. He tried turning it the other way and pushed and pulled the door in both directions. Once again, it did not move – the door was locked. Pepito stepped back and looked at the church's entire front façade. Unlike other churches, there were two other buildings attached on both sides, as though the church had been wedged between two other structures. As he looked even closer, he noticed the church's stones didn't look that old. They appeared to be cut and designed in a classic fashion in order to make the building appear more ancient, but the color and wear on the stones indicated that they had been constructed within the last few decades.

Pepito looked to his right and saw a small wooden door in the church's far right corner. He looked up. "That door probably leads to the bell tower," he thought to himself. He moved towards the door, grabbed the knob and again attempted to open it. Like the other one, this door too was locked and would not open. Pepito took a long, deep breath. He stepped away from the church and back to the edge of the top step. He examined the church's exterior closely. He surveyed the rows of grey stone stacked on top of each other, he looked carefully at the edge of the doorway and the large wooden arch that stood above it. He tilted his head and carefully studied the peak of the roof and the open topped bell tower that loomed to the right. Nothing caught his eye and nothing stood out from the ordinary. Pepito continued to peer up and down, left to right at each individual stone across the exterior, but he simply couldn't spot any signs or clues that might lead to anything.

Pepito was growing increasingly frustrated and once again he felt a pit in his stomach knowing that he had encountered an obstacle that seemed insurmountable. He sat pensively for several more minutes.

"Wait a minute," he whispered aloud. "Wait a minute... can a statue be a shrine, too? " He turned and looked back at the statue of Pachacutec. Pepito looked directly at his face. Maybe Pepito knew the secret he was attempting to say. Pepito bounced down the concrete steps and bounded over to Pachacutec. He looked down at the platform and the rows of stones. His eyes locked on the fountains. There above the water spout was a wedge-shaped opening. "I knew it!" he thought excitedly. He quickly dashed around to the other side of the foundation. He zeroed in on the second fountain – it too had a similar opening above the spout. Pepito's heart thumped loudly in his chest. He kept going – examining the remaining two sides. They also had identical openings in the same location. Pepito felt shivers run down his back. His hands shook with excitement. He lifted his left arm to retrieve the Clave pieces from the bag. He was about to pull out the first one when he heard a voice behind him. He turned and looked. There at the edge of the plaza were Cruz and Castillo. "He's at the main square by the statue, boss," blurted Cruz into his phone. Pepito gasped as the two thugs came bursting towards him.

# CHAPTER 34

Pepito shoved the Clave piece back in the bag, turned and bolted in the opposite direction of the oncoming thugs. Adrenalin shot through his veins. He held the bag tightly under his arms, like a running back carries a football, and accelerated towards the narrow street that exited the plaza ahead. He needed to put space between himself and the attackers and he needed to do it fast.

Pepito took a hard right into the street. It was an uneven, dusty road littered with potholes. The street was empty with no one around except a dog that barked loudly from behind a metal fence as Pepito darted by him. Pepito eyed the road and guided himself along a swerving route that avoided the potholes and dangerous dips. He saw a hostel on his left and considered going in to look for help, but he couldn't risk it with the thugs so close behind him.

He pushed hard up the street, still powered

by panic and fear. He could hear Cruz and Castillo grunting behind him, also negotiating the challenges of the bumpy road. Pepito continued to dash up and over the mini sinkholes in the ground. He looked ahead and noticed the road split in two different directions. To the left, the street seemed to bend and continue much like the current section – quiet and lined with more modest homes and low apartment buildings. To the right, the street cut sharply to the right and continued out of sight. "Which way? Which way?" Pepito thought anxiously. "Left looks like it goes away from town, maybe right leads back to the main parts of town where there are people to help me..." His thoughts raced through his mind and in a flash, he was pivoting hard to his right down the blind road.

Just as he came around the corner, Pepito's heart sank. He stopped abruptly to find the street led into a small cul de sac. There was a large pile of sand and dirt in the centre of the circular road and a series of attached two and three story buildings that were under construction. Pepito looked around at his options – he didn't have time to go back and try the other street. He looked back, the thugs were only a few seconds behind him.

Pepito dashed across the empty road, past the pile of soil and up to the vacant, partially finished building. He went through the entry – there were no doors or windows – and raced up the stairs to the second floor. He looked around. Several sheets of plywood were strewn across the floor, but he could see that they had been fastened down. There were also a few sections of framed walls that separated the upper floor into smaller sections. Pepito's heart thumped loudly in his chest.

"Up the stairs!" called out one of the thugs from below. In an instant, he heard boots slamming into the wooden steps below. Pepito instinctively moved into the room and leapt onto the nearest section of plywood. The board slid slightly and Pepito's feet caught on the rough lumber. His body swayed violently through the air but he managed to catch himself in time before losing his balance. The thugs were nearing the top of the stairs but he didn't dare look back – he stepped to the edge of the plywood sheet and jumped the four-foot gap to the next sheet of plywood. He braced for the wood to slide this time and quickly regained his footing. He took a few more steps and jumped again to the third and last sheet of plywood in the room. He kept moving forward to the edge of the board and the room. He put his hand out to grab the open window frame. He stuck his head out of the opening and looked out. Below him, about eight feet away, was a metal canopy- that skirted that back of the building. Pepito gasped. He turned to look back at the room and thugs behind him. They were standing, glaring at him from the top of the stairs.

"What you going to do now?" asked Castillo menacingly.

"Nowhere to go, kid," said Cruz. "Give it up. It's over."

Pepito stared back with contempt at the thugs. His eyes glowering. "How dare you," he thought to himself. "How dare you try to take what belongs to me and my people." He then spun towards the window, placed both hands on the bottom sill and jumped out the window towards the rooftop below.

The metal canopy made a loud crashing sound as Pepito slammed down hard with his hands and feet. He tumbled slightly towards the edge but quickly lifted himself upward and stabilized his feet underneath him. He looked up from where he launched himself. The two goons stood in the window frame looking down at him. Pepito clutched the bag and stepped swiftly and carefully across the canopy to the edge of the building. He reached the end where the rooftop met the adjacent building; there was only one way to go from here: down to the ground. Pepito knelt down at the edge of the metal roof and looked down. The mangled grass and shrubs were approximately nine feet below. Pepito looked back at the window – the thugs were gone. He took a deep breath, grabbed a firm hold of the eaves trough and swing his body down below the canopy. His legs dangled below and he peered down to see his feet several feet above the ground. The aluminum on the eaves trough began to bend in his hands and he heard a creak directly above his head. The light metal continued to bend and Pepito's grip began to loosen, and before he knew it, his hands let go and he dropped to the ground with a hard thud. He held tightly to his bag as he tumbled once on the small patch of grass. Pepito stood up and examined his surroundings. Across the rear yard was orange caution tape – likely marking the edge of the construction zone. He dashed across the yard towards the tape.

As Pepito ran through the bushy terrain, he could hear the thugs making their way to the rear of the building. He knew it was just a matter of seconds before they were back on his heels. As Pepito approached the yellow band of tape, he realized that it not only marked the edge of the construction site, but the property itself. The unkempt field gave way to a twenty-foot cliff that led to the street down below. While the sandy wedge was steep, Pepito was able to scamper and slide down on all fours. As he reached the bottom of the cliff, he looked up and saw the thugs peering down from overtop of the caution tape. Pepito clambered to his feet, grabbed hold of the canvas bag and darted down the street.

He was on Avenida Contisuyo, one of the main roads in the town, and as Pepito hurried down the road he came to a narrow bend. As he passed through the curve, he came upon a parked delivery van with its rear doors open. Pepito slowed down and spotted an open door leading to a small grocery store – with the appearance of people moving about inside.

"This might be my best chance," thought Pepito. He stopped running and moved to the back of the van which was directly in front of the open doorway. He looked in the storefront but he couldn't spot anyone inside. He could hear the thugs charging down the street towards him. He slid inside one of the van's open doors to conceal himself. Pepito looked down at the cargo area inside – piled directly in front of him were mesh bags filled with oranges. The thugs were near the front of the van now – rushing down the street. Pepito didn't have time to think; he grabbed a hold of one of the bags and clenched it tightly with both hands. The thugs were just a few feet away, racing along the side of the van. Pepito stepped around the door and into the road and with all his might, he swung the bag of oranges squarely into Castillo's face. The thug stopped instantly and dropped to the ground like a heavy stone. His head bounced off the cobblestones and in a flash, he was lying unconsciously on the ground.

Both Pepito and Cruz stood stunned by what had just happened. They looked down at Castillo, he seemed to be breathing but lay motionless with his eyes closed. Then Cruz turned angrily to Pepito. "You little..." he seethed. Pepito picked up the bag of oranges, swung it behind him and threw it as hard as he could towards Cruz. Cruz ducked down as the bag went sailing over his head. He then lunged at Pepito and tackled him to the ground. Pepito managed to spin to the side as Cruz grabbed hold of him and Cruz took the brunt of their crash landing on the unforgiving cobblestones. "I'm going to kill you!" yelled Cruz as he wrestled Pepito underneath him. Cruz slid on top of Pepito and held his throat with his left hand. Pepito grabbed Cruz's wrist with both hands, trying to prevent his choke hold. Cruz raised his right hand in the air, clenched it into a fist, and was about to drive it into Pepito's face when suddenly a voice yelled out, "Hey! What the hell is going in here!"

Cruz's hand froze in the air. Standing in the store's doorway, looking angry and bewildered, were two clerks. "Help me," muttered Pepito with Cruz's left hand still wrapped around his throat.

"Get off him!" ordered the middle-aged clerk with a stern and weathered face.

"Relax. This is none of your business," said Cruz slowly lifting himself off Pepito.

"It's my business now," the man shot back. He moved towards Cruz and Pepito scrambled up to his feet. The man stepped in between Cruz and Pepito and motioned for Pepito to move behind him and onto the sidewalk.

"I said this has nothing to do with you. You better step aside if you know what's good for you," warned Cruz inching backwards. But the man continued to move closer to Cruz. Out of nowhere, Cruz swung a wild punch with his right hand. The man leaned back with his head and crossed his hands in a V pattern to catch Cruz's punch. The man then locked onto Cruz's wrist, pushed down hard on his arm and forced it behind Cruz's back – forcing him to lean hard into the van's cargo bed. Cruz let out a sharp yelp from the searing pain in his right shoulder.

"I guess it's my business now, huh punk?" said the man into Cruz's ear. He then turned towards his friend in the doorway. "Quick. Call the police... looks like there is another one lying on the ground here..." The second clerk took out his phone and quickly dialed 9-1-1.

"Th... thank... thank you so much," said Pepito still trying to process the last few moments.

"No problem kid," said the man. "Don't worry. He's not going to hurt you."

The clerk hung up the phone, "They'll be here in a couple of minutes," he said. "Told me keep these guys secure until then."

"Come around and have a look at this guy," said the middle-aged man to the younger clerk. "Make sure he doesn't start something when he comes to."

The younger man stepped around the back of the van and into the street. He knelt down by Castillo. "He's breathing. Got a big welt on his face, but still breathing."

"Good. Keep an eye on him," said the man. "Hey kid, why was this guy trying to hurt you?" He turned and looked back at the storefront, "Hey kid..." But he only found an empty sidewalk; Pepito had already vanished down the street.

# CHAPTER 35

Pepito continued down Avenida Contisuy-o until he reached the river. He heard drums and excited crowd noises to his left. He looked down Avenida Imperio de los Incas, a swell of people had gathered on the sidewalks. Pepito stepped into the street and watched as, way off in the distance, a group of musicians walked in unison in the centre of the avenue. The solstice parade had begun and was making its way down the broad street that hugged the river. Pepito wished that, for a moment, he could take in the parade – he loved these types of celebrations.

But he couldn't stay and his focus shifted back to the precious stones in his shoulder bag. He turned and began walking north on Avenido Imperio de los Incas. He picked up the pace – rushing up the street for several hundred metres, he turned right and then followed the same route he had taken some thirty minutes ago.

Moments later, Pepito reached the main plaza's outer boundary. He focused in on the statue of Pachacutec as it stood shining brightly in the centre of the square. The plaza was eerily quiet and vacant – not a soul around. Pepito strode with confidence towards the statue – he knew that the treasure was near, he could feel it in his bones.

He reached the base of the statue and peered up at Pachacutec's majestic image. "I think I know your secret, my friend," Pepito whispered softly. He reached into his bag, and for the second time, pulled out one of the Clave pieces. Despite all the running and reckless actions from the past few days, the stone was still intact, devoid of any damage.

Pepito exhaled slowly. "This is it," he thought. He stepped towards the base of the statue, and with the narrow portion pointing forward, extended the Clave piece into the space above the spewing fountain. The piece slid in perfectly. Pepito's heart bounced in his chest and he let out a quick gasp. "I can't believe it..." he thought.

His hands shook again as he pulled a second Clave piece from the bag. He quickly shuffled to the other side of the foundation wall. He steadied his hand and reached across the narrow moat. Again, he positioned the Clave piece so it would fit in the opening; and it did – another perfect fit. Pepito was bouncing with excitement. "Two more," he thought.

He scrambled over to the third foundation wall. A light breeze was picking up and as Pepito readied the third piece, some dust kicked up from the ground; forcing him to close his eyes momentarily. After a moment, the wind died down and Pepito inched towards the fountain. The wind continued and blew some of the water from the fountain at the stone, but Pepito leaned forward and set the stone in the third opening. "Just one more..."

Pepito turned to the final wall and fountain. He took a long deep breath and exhaled slowly. He reached into the canvas bag and pulled out the last Clave piece. He looked at it closely; carefully examining the details of the shapes and lines. He couldn't believe how familiar the map seemed now compared to when he first saw it two days ago. He raised the Clave piece triumphantly in front of himself and began to move forward towards the foundation wall.

"That's far enough," called out a voice behind him. Pepito spun around quickly on his heels. He looked around to find the source of the voice. The square was empty in all directions. Then, from the shadows of a doorway, out stepped Cica into the afternoon sun.

"Well, well, well... look how far you've come, little man," snarled Cica. "Very impressive. Very impressive," Cica said moving towards Pepito and the statue. Pepito took a step back, his breath caught in his throat. "You didn't think I would just let you take what is mine, did you?"

taunted Cica. "You have caused me a lot of trouble and now you owe me big time... and as everyone knows, when you owe Cica, he's going to come for you and it's going to be payback time..."

Pepito's pulse raced and his heart thundered in his chest. His shoulders heaved up and down as he tried to catch his breath. "This..." he stammered, "this doesn't belong to you."

"Really?" said Cica disdainfully; he was now just twenty or so feet away from Pepito. "You don't remember stealing it from me in my office? Maybe a few shots to the head will help jog your memory." Cica was close enough now that Pepito could see the scar on his face and the malice in his eyes.

"You stole it first," Pepito shot back between clenched teeth.

"Maybe... but right now I'm the judge and I'm the jury...and I say give me the stone," Cica said holding out his right hand.

Pepito looked at his coarse fingers with contempt. "This is not how it's supposed to end," he thought. "He can't win..."

"Now!" seethed Cica. "Give me the stone or, I swear, I will beat you to death and let you die like a dog in street."

Cica lowered his outstretched hand and clenched both his fists; his eyes were ablaze with rage and his teeth gnashed under his curled upper lip. Pepito froze. He had never seen such rage in another person before. He feared for his safety like never before. He looked down at the Clave piece and then back up at Cica. He knew he had no other option.

"Now," Cica said impatiently. Pepito lifted his hand and the stone hesitantly towards Cica.

"Smart move," said Cica, swiping the stone from Pepito's hand, "You just saved yourself a serious beating." Pepito stepped to the side as Cica strode to the final opening above the fountain. Cica fumbled with the Clave piece, trying to determine which way to insert it. He reached out and tried to place it in the opening but it didn't fit. Cica pulled it back out, turned it 90 degrees to the left and tried again. This time the stone slid in smoothly.

Cica and Pepito stood there motionless, waiting. But nothing happened. Cica looked over at Pepito and then back again at the Clave piece. Cica leaned forward and pushed the stone further into the wall. Suddenly, the water in the fountain stopped. Then a slow, grinding sound emerged from the centre of the statue's foundation. The sound began to grow in intensity and became louder and more intense. Both Cica and Pepito took a step backwards. The statue began to shake slightly and then the stone foundation itself began to vibrate, with dust and dirt falling from the mortar down to the ground. Pepito stood watching, mouth agape.

The wall directly in front of them began to shake, followed by a loud, metallic jangle; like a large bolt released from its latch. Pepito watch in awe as the wall began to move – sliding downward below the ground. The entire wall, about four feet high and six feet wide, moved in one piece, slowly and deliberately under the foundation structure.

"Woah," said Pepito softly. The wall stopped once the top edge reached the edge of the moat that bordered the structure. The afternoon sun was placed conveniently at their backs and provided them with light into the new-found cavity.

Cica moved quickly to the open space and peered inside. "What the..." he muttered aloud. Cica lowered his head and upper body and stepped into the cavity. Pepito couldn't see what lay beyond but by Cica's advancing movement, it appeared that there was a staircase leading downward. Cica landed after only a few steps – Pepito raced over to have a look and craned his head into the opening. Cica turned and looked back up at Pepito, "Get the hell out of here, kid. Don't even think of coming down," he ordered menacingly.

Pepito pulled back in frustration. He didn't get much of a look – but what he did see resembled a basement cold cellar. The space looked empty, but he only had a partial view. Pepito could hear Cica moving about in the secret room. He appeared to be rummaging about and Pepito could see faint light coming from what he assumed was Cica's phone.

Pepito wanted to badly go into the room and look for himself but he knew Cica would turn violent if he did. His vexation was gnawing away at him, but he was able to control his emotions while he waited anxiously.

"Where the hell is everything?" Cica suddenly thundered from below.

Pepito stiffened, "What does he mean?" Pepito wondered, "There is nothing down there?" Then Cica shuffled to the bottom of the stairs and began stepping forcefully up each step. In an instant, his head emerged in the opening and he lifted himself out from the hidden space; his hand clutching a shiny plate sized object.

"So much for your father and his glorious job, kid... this is a joke... he's a joke and you're a joke..." Cica said scornfully. Pepito was stunned. He didn't know what to make of Cica, his words, and the object he was holding. Cica came face to face with Pepito – he was about to grab Pepito by the scruff of his sweater when a loud whirring sound interrupted his progress.

Cica spun around. Coming towards them was a police car with its blue lights flashing from the rooftop. Pepito breathed a huge sigh of relief. Cica's face clenched, "Son of a..." he muttered through clenched teeth. The police car drove through the square and stopped abruptly just a few metres from Cica and Pepito. Three doors swung open and out of the car sprung Officer Nunes, Senhor Gonzalez, and Marta.

"Pepito!" Marta called out. "You okay?" Pepito smiled slightly and nodded. The police officer held out his left hand and placed his right hand over his gun holster.

"Just stay right there," he ordered to Cica. "Don't move... just stay right where you are."

Cica raised his empty hand in the air and smiled menacingly at the young cop, "Relax, officer... no need to get excited. Everything is cool here...we're just talking..."

Senhor Gonzalez moved towards Marta and put his hands protectively on her shoulders.

"What are you doing here? What business do you have here? With this boy?" asked Officer Nunes, releasing the clasp on his gun holster.

Cica rolled his eyes. "When are you people going to learn to stay out of my damned..." Suddenly, Cica hurled the golden object from his hand towards the officer. The cop raised his left armed to shield himself as the object bounced off his forearm – he pulled the gun from his hip and pointed it directly at Cica. "Don't move!" he yelled.

Cica tilted his head to the side menacingly. He looked over at Senhor Gonzalez and Marta and then back at the cop. "What are you going to do, shoot me?"

The officer's gun quivered in the air and his legs began to shake underneath him. "Don't force me to... don't you..." he said now gripping the gun with both hands.

"I think you need to put the gun away before you hurt yourself," said Cica taking a step toward the novice officer.

"Don't move... I said... don't move," he said. But Cica continued to move forward; just a few feet separated them. Cica took one more step – the officer pulled the gun to his side and then swung the gun directly at Cica's head. Cica threw up both his arms in defense as the gun banged off his left wrist and went flying in the air behind him. Cica growled loudly and pushed hard into the police officer' chest, sending him tumbling backwards on the cobblestones.

Cica spun around looking for the errant gun. It had fallen in the narrow moat that surrounded the foundation wall. Cica knelt down on all fours to retrieve it from the water trough. Marta looked at Cica as he searched hastily. Acting instinctively, Marta burst away from Senhor Gonzalez and made a bee line towards Cica. Just like she had many times before on soccer goal kicks, Marta took three hard strides and just as Cica pulled the gun from the trough, she kicked him as hard as she could squarely on the side of his midsection, cracking two of his ribs.

Cica cried out in pain, and then curled up into a ball, clutching his side as the gun dropped out of his hand and onto the ground beside him.

"Marta!" called out Senhor Gonzalez. She stepped back from Cica and Senhor Gonzalez moved in between them, he then reached down and picked up the fallen gun. Pepito rushed to Marta's side. The young officer scrambled to his feet and dashed towards Cica. The officer pulled out hand cuffs from his belt, grabbed Cica's right wrist and secured the cuff tightly around it. Cica again cried out in pain from the knife-like sensation in his ribs. The officer put his knee down on Cica's back and tightened the second cuff around Cica's other wrist. Senhor Gonzalez handed the gun back to the cop and Officer Nunes pointed it firmly above the prone thug.

# CHAPTER 36

Pepito, Marta, and Senhor Gonzalez watched as Officer Nunes ushered Cica into the back of his police cruiser.

"Give me some time to call this in to the station. We will need to wait for backup to take you three to the station," said the officer as he slid into the front seat and reached for the radio remote. Marta turned eagerly to Pepito, "What happened here? Where have you been? Is that the guy that took you in the plaza?"

Pepito sighed deeply. "It's a long story and I promise to tell you everything, but right now we need to finish this," he said gesturing to the opening in the statue's base.

"Pepito, did the Clave lead you here?" asked Senhor Gonzalez.

"Yes... I am so close – I just know it... just trust me for a minute and come with me." Pepito bent down and picked up the object Cica brought from the hidden room - a fabric covered disc with a metal handle - he then took a few steps forward to the edge of the cavity. "In here, let's go." He grabbed the handrail at the side of the staircase and stepped down the nine steps that led to the floor. Marta and Senhor Gonzalez followed him down. The sun poured into the entrance, but much of the space remained covered in darkness.

"Can we use the light from your phone?" Pepito asked Senhor Gonzalez.

"Sure..." Senhor Gonzalez replied pulling the phone from his pocket. He held it out to illuminate the area in front of them. The secret room was approximately 20 feet long and 20 feet wide. The walls were made of cinder block and surrounded the dusty concrete floor. Most disturbing to Pepito, however, was that the room was empty. Nothing was visible anywhere.

Pepito shook his head in confusion, "This is supposed to be the end," he wondered aloud. " This is supposed to be the Casa's location."

Senhor Gonzalez turned to Pepito, "The Clave may have brought you here but this could be an old location. It's possible that it's been moved from here." he said.

"But I don't have any more clues... this is supposed to... wait," he thought suddenly. "There might be something in here to guide us... let's look closely."

Senhor Gonzalez moved closer to the far wall and shone his phone up and down the eight-foot high wall. "There are different coloured mortar lines here... looks like these walls were put up at different times," he said.

"Why do you think that is? asked Marta.

"It could be that this room was bigger at one point, or led to other rooms... maybe even a tunnel... it's hard to tell..."

Marta looked up at the ceiling, "Hey, I see something - there is something written up there," she said excitedly.

Pepito and Senhor Gonzalez hurried to the centre of the room where Marta stood. Senhor Gonzalez tilted his phone and aimed it at the ceiling. They three of them looked up. Inscribed in the concrete ceiling was the following:
"On Clean grounds we stand to see further."

Marta read the phrase aloud. "What do you think it means?" she asked.

Senhor Gonzalez thought for a moment. "Well..." he began, "it does resemble a famous phrase."

He tilted his head and pressed his lips together wondering if there in fact was a connection. "The phrase," he continued, "is from Isaac Newton... he once said 'if I have seen further it is by standing on the shoulders of giants' and it means that his achievements were possible because he learned from all the great scientists before him...but I don't know if this quotation refers to that..."

This must be a clue, though," said Pepito. "I found another message carved in stone before... wait a second." Pepito looked down at the object in his hand. "Look further... clean grounds... clean grounds..." He knelt down and pressed the object down on the floor with the fabric side touching the dirt covered concrete floor. He began to slide the object along the ground from side to side. After several strokes, he had cleared a small area, removing the light layer of dirt and dust. Pepito pulled his hand back – he gasped with delight. On the ground before him were segments of painted lines, both curved and straight.

"I knew it!" Pepito exclaimed. He knelt back down and continued to swipe away at the dirt – revealing more lines and images.

"Wow, Pepito," said Marta excitedly. "That's amazing!" She reached for her hooded sweatshirt that she commonly wore around her waist and untied it from her hips. She quickly bent down and started to clear away the dirt beneath her with her sweatshirt. Pepito glanced across at her.

"Hey, don't use that – it's your favourite hoodie," he said.

"Don't worry, you can buy me a new one," Marta responded with a smile.

Senhor Gonzalez pulled out a handkerchief and helped with the floor wiping efforts. Within moments they had exposed a large section of the ground, revealing a large, rectangular image. Pepito stood up and examined their progress. "Looks like we need to clear just a little bit more in this corner," he said pointing to his left. The three hastily wiped the area he was referring to. "Okay, I think that's good. I think we got most of it," Pepito said. He lifted himself up again and moved to the staircase by the entrance. He took several steps up and then turned back to look down at the image on the floor. His mouth opened wide.

"What is it? What do you see?" Marta asked eagerly.

"Here. This should help," said Senhor Gonzalez lifting his phone above the painted lines.

Pepito looked at the full and complete image – taking in all the details and features. He leaned his head forward as he spotted a specific marking in the bottom part of the drawing. He closed his eyes and smiled.

"What?" repeated Marta. "Tell us!"

"It's a map," Pepito finally said softly. "The map of this area, all around here." He pointed to the centre of the image, "Look here, these hills – this is Machu Picchu... and this small grid over here – that's the town of Aguas, where we are... and here is the river... and these are the other mountains... and of course," he chuckled to himself, "of course, this here... this right here," he said pointing to a small X in the lower left side of the drawing, "this... this marks the spot to... the Casa del Oro."

"And you know where this is?" asked Senhor Gonzalez.

Pepito let out a deep sigh. "I do... I know exactly where that is." He shook his head again and smiled contently.

"Well don't be a bonehead – take us there," said Marta, a little annoyed with Pepito's coyness.

"Yeah... okay... don't worry. I will share everything with you." Pepito suddenly thought about his mom and dad – it had been hours since they heard from him. "I need to call my mom – can I please borrow your phone?"

Senhor Gonzalez handed the phone to Pepito. "Come on," he said guiding Marta towards the stairs, "let's give him some privacy." Senhor Gonzalez and Marta began to make their way up the stairs.

"Hey," said Pepito. "How did you know where to find me?"

"We figured you were looking for the Casa and came to Machu Picchu to find you," said Marta.

"We arrived late so went to the police for assistance... luckily two men were arrested and they told the police that you might be here," said Senhor Gonzalez.

"Wow," whispered Pepito, shaking his head.

"We will leave you be for now..." Senhor Gonzalez and Marta continued to make their way up the stairs and out through the opening. The sun still shone brightly between the surrounding buildings. Another police cruiser had arrived and Officer Nunes and two other officers were talking animatedly behind the vehicles.

"I guess we will have to go with them now and give our statements," said Senhor Gonzalez.

"Let's do it quickly, though," said Marta. "We

have a house of gold to find."

Pepito stepped halfway up the stairs with his head emerging in the opening, "Are the police still here?" he asked.

"Yes, two more have arrived," answered Senhor Gonzalez.

"Well, tell them to forget the station," said Pepito determinedly, "we have to go the hospital..."

# CHAPTER 37

Pepito rushed into the front door of the modest medical clinic. Following close behind him were Marta and Senhor Gonzalez. Waiting at the front reception area was Rosita. Pepito and Rosita saw each other and immediately grabbed one another in a warm embrace.

"Pepito, I'm so happy you're okay," Rosita said clutching him tightly. "I was so worried there..."

"I'm sorry I made you worry," Pepito responded. "I really didn't mean to."

"I know. But you're safe now and that's all that matters," she said lifting her head back from his. "Ready to see your father?" Pepito nodded. "He's in here," she said motioning down the hall. Then suddenly Rosita realized that Pepito did not come alone, "Marta! My goodness – you're here, too... Senhor Gonzalez, hello... I had no idea that -"

"We came to help, Mrs. Capac. Sorry to be intruding right now, we just came to assist Pepito." said Senhor Gonzalez.

"Thank you. Thank you so much for everything you've done. I'm just so glad that everyone is safe now."

"We have so much to tell you!" Marta said excitedly.

"I can't wait to hear all about it," Rosita said with a warm smile.

"We will leave for now, though," said Senhor Gonzalez putting his arm around Marta.

"Thank you. We won't be long," replied Rosita as she and Pepito turned to walk down the hallway.

Inside the small examination room, Jose sat on a long table with a square white bandage over his right temple. Rosita and Pepito stepped inside.

Jose looked up, "Pepito!" He sprung up from the table and stepped forward. Jose pulled Pepito in and hugged him. His arms wrapping securely around his son. They stood in silence for a moment as Rosita stood in the doorway, wiping the tears from her face.

"We've been trying to call you all morning," Jose said. "You didn't answer the phone."

"I know... I couldn't... the guys – those thugs came after me...and I had to leave..." Pepito responded.

Jose pulled himself back, placing his hands on Pepito's upper arms. Jose looked closely into Pepito's eyes. "Did you take the Clave with you?" he asked. Pepito nodded; his eyes sparkled and a small smile formed in the corners of his mouth.

Jose drew his breath in, "You know, don't you?" he asked.

Pepito's eyes widened. "Yes... I think... I think I do." A proud smile spread across Jose's face; he shook his head from side to side.

"I always felt deep inside that this day would come... but I never imagined you would be this young..." Jose reached up and put his right hand behind Pepito's head. "I'm so proud of you...you have no idea."

"I'm proud of you too, Papa..." Pepito said as his eyes began to well up.

"Come, we need to get out of here," Jose said turning himself towards Rosita. "I don't need to wait for the test results – I'm fine."

"Are you sure?" asked Rosita. "What about the doctor?"

"I'm okay - we need to go...we've been apart long enough... I want to hear everything, okay Pepito? Every last detail."

Pepito nodded. "Can we get something to eat, though? I'm starving!"

"Of course, my love" said Rosita grabbing Pepito's hand. The family then left the exam room and headed back to the main lobby.

An hour later, Jose, Rosita, and Pepito stood side by side some twenty feet in front of the farm house. Senhor Gonzalez and Marta stood just a few feet behind them. They all looked straight at the building, captivated by its vision. Pepito put his hands on his hips and breathed in a long, contented sigh. Rosita put her hand on his shoulder.

"So... this is it..." Pepito said finally. "After all that running and chasing and..." He shook his head with delight. "It was here, right here... the whole time." Jose lifted his arm and placed it on Pepito's other shoulder. "So how far does it go, Papa?" asked Pepito.

"Well it fills the lower foundation and part of the wall on the first floor," responded Jose.

"Wow – even the walls, too. That's amazing," said Pepito. "I should have known when I was in the crawl space under the bed... the walls were so smooth... I should have noticed it then..."

"It's painted down there so it wouldn't be obvious," said Rosita reassuringly.

"So what happens next?" asked Pepito.

"Now we have to take you, well... all three of you," Jose said turning to Marta and Senhor Gonzalez. "And we have to meet with the President and the executive council. You will need to be sworn in as honorary private officers. And all of you will need to take an oath of service and confidentiality." He looked at Marta, "Are you up for it?"

"You can count on me, Mr. Capac," Marta replied eagerly.

"Senhor Gonzalez?" asked Jose. "What do you think?"

"It would be an honour, sir," said Senhor Gonzalez.

"Excellent," said Jose. He then turned and faced Pepito. "What do you think? Are you ready to be a Shadow Runner?"

Pepito smiled widely, "Are you kidding me, Papa? I already am one..."

# EPILOGUE

For hundreds of years, from the late 1400s to the early 1900s, the site of Machu Picchu was abandoned and lost to the outside world. For over four centuries the city slowly deteriorated and became overgrown with wild grass and bushes. Only the nearby locals knew of its existence. During this time, the precious golden artifacts in the Casa Del Oro collection were kept in a single location hidden deep in the mountains surrounding Machu Picchu. The clues beyond the Northern Gate indicated its precise location.

In 1911, an American explorer named Hiram Bingham, after years of searching, came upon the holy city and "discovered" the lost city of Machu Picchu. Restoration efforts began and soon after, people from around the world began visiting. After a few decades, the site became one of the world's greatest tourist destinations. However, as the tourists arrived, so did the treasure hunters in search of the Casa Del Oro. As more and more people poked around the ruins and the surrounding area looking for the Casa, it was moved to an ancient holy site in Aguas Calientes in the

1960s. Approximately twenty years later, the church was built on that site and the golden treasures were to be placed in a secret underground room in the basement.

Unfortunately, during the construction phase, a massive mudslide occurred at the base of the mountain where the church was being built. Tonnes of mud, rock, and construction materials came crashing down on the golden artifacts. After many days and hours of painstaking work, the ruble was cleared and the golden pieces were recovered. But the damage was done. Almost every item was damaged beyond repair. Beautiful swords, shields, and headdresses now looked like tangled, distorted props from a horror movie. Around the same time, the statue of Pachacutec was being built nearby. The mangled artifacts, as well as the floor map, were placed in the statue's foundation for temporary safe keeping. Those in charge of protecting the Casa Del Oro were very distraught with what had happened and unsure of what to do next.

The President held a series of secret meetings with his closest government officials, and it was decided that for security and restoration purposes, the gold would be melted into several large rectangular sections. This would prevent any thieves from taking individual items and would also allow the government to transport the gold in the future, if need be.

The gold was melted and reshaped in a

nearby factory under the close watch of military personnel and then transported to a remote plot of land some five kilometres from Machu Picchu. A hole for the foundation was dug and the gold was placed, section by section, in the hole. A simple farm house was then built on top of the golden foundation. This modest home, the house made from gold - the Casa Del Oro, has remained intact to this day.

Made in the USA
Middletown, DE
02 May 2020